LAND OF
PROMISE

BOOK 8

LAND OF PROMISE

T. L. TEDROW

SCHOLASTIC INC.
New York Toronto London Auckland Sydney

Illustrations by Dennas Davis

ISBN 0-590-22655-X

12 11 10 9 8 7 6 5 4 3 2 1   5 6 7 8 9/9 0/0

Printed in the U.S.A.   40

First Scholastic printing, April 1995

To my pretty wife Carla and our younguns,
C.T., Tyler, Tara and Travis.

May we never forget the magic of childhood dreams which
is really what being young at heart is all about.

And to my good friends at Thomas Nelson,
for making these dreams come true.

Contents

FOREWORD

Laura Ingalls Wilder is loved the world over for her pioneer books and the wonderful television series that was based on them. Though much has been written about the Old West, it was Laura Ingalls Wilder who brought the frontier to life for millions of young readers.

The Laura Ingalls Wilder story did not stop after her last book. She and her husband, Manly, and daughter, Rose, moved to Mansfield, Missouri, from South Dakota in 1894. Laura was 27, Manly 38, Rose seven. They arrived with only one hundred dollars to their name and the few possessions they had salvaged from their house that had burned down.

They used the money as a down payment on a broken-down farm, and after a decade of hard work they had built the finest house Laura had ever lived in, which I have given the name Apple Hill Farm.

Laura Ingalls Wilder went on to become a pioneer journalist in Mansfield, Missouri, where for sixteen years she was a columnist for the farm family weekly *Missouri Ruralist*. She spoke her mind about the environment, land abuse, women's rights, the consequences of war, and she observed the march of progress as cars, planes, radios, and new inventions changed America forever.

While this book is a fictional account of Laura's exploits, it retains the historical integrity of her columns, diary, family background, personal beliefs, and the general history of the times in which she lived. However, any references to specific events, real people, or real places are intended only to give the fiction a setting in historical reality. Names, characters, and incidents are either the product of the author's imagination or are used fictitiously, and their resemblance, if any, to real-life counterparts is purely coincidental.

T. L. Tedrow

CHAPTER 1

A Promise Is a Promise

The beauty of the Ozarks surrounded them. Laura shook her hair loose to catch the breeze. "This has been a wonderful day," she laughed, smiling at her husband, Manly. He hummed a tune.

"Hold on," he said, gripping the steering wheel of the Oldsmobile. Laura reached for the door handle, but was too late and slid over against Manly as the car swerved wildly.

Straightening the car out, Manly put his arm around her. "I used to try that same thing when we courted in the buggy. Remember?"

"How could I forget!" She laughed and pecked him on the cheek.

Manly sneaked a kiss on her mouth. "How do you stay so pretty?"

"It's something I have to work at every day." She smiled, and turned to look out the window at the houses they passed.

Their small town of Mansfield was surrounded by family farms of newly arrived and second- and third-generation arrivals to America. Wright County seemed like a patchwork quilt of the globe. A place where you could hear a smattering of Scandinavian or French as easily as German or a thick Irish brogue.

Manly was still humming the foot-stomping fiddle and harmonica tunes that Blindman Thomas had played at the impromptu concert at the town square. "That old black man can really play, you know it?"

"I just can't imagine how he plays without seeing," said Laura.

Manly eased the car around the turn as they approached the Willow Creek Bridge. "Just practice, I guess."

Manly tooted his horn and waved to a neighbor. "Blindman's grandson, Reever, said that Blindman can play any song he hears. It's a God-given gift."

Laura nodded. "Did you see the way the people reacted?" she asked.

Manly laughed. "They all seemed happier than dogs in a meat-packing house," he laughed. "Thought I'd never see the day when you could mix a bunch of hard-shell Baptists, Catholics, Methodists, and Irish in the same room and get a consensus on anything."

Manly sang out a square dance song that Blindman had played. "You swing Sal and I'll swing Kate. Hurry up, boys, don't be late."

"Chan seemed to like it too," Laura added.

"Chan likes anythin' that's free," Manly said. "He's as tight as a frog's hind end."

"He's just frugal. That's how he's done so well."

Manly laughed. "And Dr. George was doin' some jumpin' and dancin'. I liked it when he swung Miss Polly around."

"Everyone was clapping for them."

"That big woman's a great dancer," he said, then paused. "I thought Dr. George and Bentley were going to have words when Blindman sang out, 'Blackfolk raise the cotton and whitefolk keep the dough'."

"I guess the truth hurts," Laura frowned, then grimaced.

"Maybe you need to rest or something," Manly said, concerned.

Laura nodded. "I do feel kind of tired . . . sort of drained."

"You still got the sick stomach?" Manly asked, pulling into their driveway.

"It just comes and goes."

"Maybe you ought to clean your blood with some molasses and sulphur. Or maybe you ought to drink some salt tonic and take a nap." Laura looked at him like he was crazy. "I know!" Manly exclaimed. "What you need is some skunk oil."

"Skunk oil? Whatever are you talking about?"

"Just one of the home remedies I heard the boys talkin' 'bout down at the feed store."

"The remedy sounds worse than the sickness," Laura said, shaking her head.

Manly shrugged. "You're the one feelin' sick. Me, why I'd consider drinkin' some skunk oil to get myself feelin' better."

"Manly Wilder, if you ever start drinking skunk oil, you'll be sleeping in the barn."

"You up to eatin' dinner?" he laughed. "Those fish I caught this morning have my name written all over them," he smiled.

Laura laughed, realizing that he had been playing with her. "What I can't eat won't go to waste with you around."

"Yes sir," Manly said, wishing he was back on the river, "that johnboat of mine just sneaks into the eddies. I get the biggest fish by catchin' 'em by surprise."

Laura looked at him, shaking her head at his enthusiasm. "Did you really give old Mr. Bentley the big bass you caught?"

Manly shrugged. "He did the paddling and hadn't caught much of a thing."

"But you gave him the biggest fish you said you ever caught."

"You got to keep your word," Manly said. "I told him that if I caught one bigger than all the rest, why, I'd give it to him."

"And then you caught the biggest one you've ever landed."

"It was the biggest one I've ever seen 'round these parts."

"I'm surprised he took it."

Manly shrugged. "He didn't want to, but heck, I already had a bucket of perch, so I just gave it to him." He paused and looked at Laura. "A promise is a promise."

CHAPTER 2

AUTUMN OF OUR LIVES

Manly squeezed her hand. "It's a good life we got, and don't you ever forget." He grinned as he opened the door and kissed her lightly on the cheek.

"I appreciate it every day." She nodded and walked through the door to the kitchen. "Things are so safe and secure here."

"Best place in the world to raise a kid," Manly nodded. "Did I tell you what Dr. George told me?" he said, putting the coffee water on the stove.

"What?"

"Said that the hill women tell their daughters on their wedding night that they can expect to have a baby every two years until they're forty." Manly whistled in astonishment. "Can you imagine that?"

"Do you wish we'd had another child?" Laura asked, suddenly wondering if he was trying to tell her something.

"Naw, Honeybee, Rose has been enough to handle. Now that she's away to college, it's just goin' to be you and me around the old place."

Laura looked out the window toward the orchards of her

beloved Apple Hill Farm. "We could always adopt. I've read that there are dozens of children needing homes at the Springfield State Orphanage."

Manly came up behind and hugged her. "Rose had such big blue eyes and golden hair, didn't she?" Manly asked, remembering his baby girl.

"She was a fat and happy baby," Laura nodded at the memory. In DeSmet life wasn't filled with the good fortune they had now. It brought back sad memories.

Manly opened the door. "I better run back to the barn and put out some more feed. I'll be back in a bit."

Laura stood in the doorway. She looked at the ruggedly handsome face of her husband of twenty years. *You wanted a house full of kids, but we only had one. Rose. We lost the son you wanted so badly.* For a moment, a wave of depression swept over Laura, but she shook it off.

Ma said that women sometimes get sad when they know that life's changing on them. When they see their own children growing up and ready to have children. That's when we realize that we're entering the autumn of our lives. Laura paused. *The autumn of our lives.*

Laura watched Manly limp away, remembering the stroke that he'd suffered. Suddenly, she closed her eyes, trying to block out the memory of their house burning down . . . losing the crops . . . forced to live off the generosity of relatives.

We didn't starve, but times were tough. We always had clothes, some of them hand-me-downs, but so did a lot of folks. We fought off sickness and death with only our home remedies because we couldn't afford the doctor. I guess it was our faith that pulled us through . . . and our hope in the future.

Laura looked off, nodding at how much they had depended on faith. *Our work was never-ending, just as our crops seemed never to come up right. But we tried to stay happy. Just had our homemade fun and ourselves. Waiting for the joy of new birth . . . waiting for a new . . .*

And then a scene from her life came back to her. She stared off toward the horizon. The shadows seemed to lengthen around the house. The old midwife was holding a baby boy. Her baby boy. It was the summer of 1889.

It was as if she were floating above the memory, stepping back in time. Manly held the spitting image of himself in his arms, carrying him around the room. *I've never seen a prouder man,* Laura thought.

Laura lay in the bed exhausted from giving birth. She looked at the tiny face of her baby as the midwife handed him to her. Suddenly, Laura was alarmed. "What have you done to my baby?" she asked. "Why is his face yellow?"

"Somethin' wrong?" Manly asked, hovering by the side of the bed.

"There is nothin' wrong," the midwife said defensively.

"Then why is he yellow?" asked Laura.

"I just washed him in egg, to make his skin soft." Laura started to get up but the midwife held her down. "You shouldn't be moving."

"I'm going to wash the egg off," Laura said.

"I'll do it," the midwife said, leaving the room.

In a few moments she returned, handing Laura her freshly scrubbed baby boy. While Laura tried to nurse the baby, the old woman began cleaning up her things, telling Laura to begin her lying-in period. "Got to let your insides get back in place," she instructed. The midwife looked at Manly. "She is to lie here for nine or ten days. You do the housework."

The old woman paused, then smiled at the baby. "This may be the only vacation you'll ever have. Use the ten days to build up your strength."

Laura kissed the baby's cheek, nodding. The midwife went on: "I've had six babies myself and I stayed in bed for ten days with each of 'em. That's why I'm so strong. Well, good-bye and God bless," she said, leaving Laura in the small two-room claim house.

"He looks just like you, Manly," Laura remembered saying.

"Times are gettin' better, ain't they, girl?" Manly said, hugging the baby to his chest. "What are we goin' to name the baby?" he asked, kissing the boy's cheek.

"Let's just wait a bit. A name will come to us," Laura heard herself say from the bed.

But we didn't name the baby. In twelve days our son was dead. We made the grim journey together to the cemetery southwest of town. It was just this side of the Reverend Brown's land claim.

She remembered Manly standing by the tiny grave, holding his hands up in prayer. "A little time on earth he spent, 'til God for him his angel sent."

"You got to accept it, Laura," her father told her at the graveside. "Sometimes there's a natural shortness of life with its own natural end."

Laura felt her knees give way as the racking sobs overtook her. *We laid our baby boy to rest without a name. Just a nameless limestone head marker that said nothing but screamed out everything about what was happening to our lives.*

"Hey, Laura," Manly shouted out, as he glanced across the yard and through the screen door. "You look like you've seen a ghost. Somethin' wrong?"

"No," Laura said quietly, coming back to the moment, "just thinking."

Manly limped toward the house. "Well, just be glad that we don't have a pack of young'uns runnin' around here." He smiled. "I don't think I could keep up with 'em at my age."

"Do you wish you had a son?" Laura asked weakly.

Manly saw the look in her eye and knew what she had been thinking about. "Laura, if the good Lord had meant for me to have a son, he would have done it. But we got a beautiful daughter and we got ourselves. What more could a man ask for?"

"You keep talking like we're old. We could still be good parents."

He hugged Laura tightly, then laughed. "Laura, my pap used to tell me that we're all just diamonds in the rough, and when the Lord rolls us around long enough and we're polished, he'll take us home."

"Well," she smiled, "you've certainly got a lot more time."

"Why's that?"

"'Cause I can't see a bit of polish on you," she kidded him.

"Is there anything more you'd want right now, girl?"

Laura smiled, forcing away the sad thoughts. "Well, for some reason, I wish I had a jar of peaches."

"Peaches? You want me to get you some up from the cellar?"

"That's sweet of you, but we used the last jar of them for the Sunday meal."

"How 'bout I run to town and get you some?"

"I just have this craving for some peaches, that's all," she said quietly, feeling a bit weak.

"Well, I got a cravin' for those fish I caught. Let's bread 'em up and fry 'em fast," he laughed.

CHAPTER 3

VOICES PAST AND PRESENT

On the other side of town, someone else was absorbed by memories. Edward Gorman, a former sergeant in the U.S. Army, sat in his dank and dirty two-room cabin. Smoke from the cigarette clamped between his fingers curled around his head.

His thoughts were thousands of miles away. At the port of Tientsin in China. In his mind it was again July 13, 1900, when the U.S. government had sent troops to put down the Boxer Rebellion. Though it was a short-lived war, it had been hard-fought and costly to the allies who joined together to fight to keep their trading interests open.

Gorman had lost a leg in the final battle. He had been shot several times as he tried to keep the U.S. flag in the air. His mentor and father-figure, Colonel Liscum, had died moments later.

I was sent to defend our national interests, Gorman thought, puffing on his cigarette. *I was fightin' along side of Brits, Krauts, Frenchies, I-talians, Japs, and the Austrians.*

His mood darkened. He remembered the fear that had gone up and down the lines of defense with the rumors of what the Chinese did to those they captured alive. Gorman still carried the suicide knife he'd planned to use if he was captured.

The sound of gunfire erupted in his mind. Gorman stood up on his good leg, swinging his arms from side to side. He thought he was back on the battlefield again.

"Colonel! Colonel Liscum! They're comin'!" Gorman called out to the empty room.

Then it all faded away. His arms fell back to his side. Gorman watched the dust in the room swirl around him. *I need some air. Think I'll go to the store and get some supplies.*

At Bedal's General Store, Gorman stood in line waiting to pay for the coffee and sugar he had weighed out of the fifty-pound sacks in the back. Stalks of bananas hung overhead, which was the only fresh fruit that Bedal sold. Most local people grew their own fruits and vegetables.

A cold potbellied stove, two chairs, and a checkerboard set on a barrel stood alone in the back corner. The long glass counters, built-in flour bins, a millinery, and dressing rooms to try on the ready-made clothes lined the walls.

The people already in line had given their list of items they needed to Lafayette Bedal as they walked in, and were now waiting for him to package it up when they got to the counter. Gorman was the only one who insisted upon gathering everything himself.

The ruddy-faced war veteran with ruddy drinker's cheeks looked around at the sacks of dried peaches from California and the wooden wheels of cheddar and longhorn cheese. Gorman wished he had the money for a hunk of the cheddar but had grown used to doing without. *The war in China made me poor,* he thought. *Made it so I couldn't farm and earn a normal livin'.*

He looked at the people in line and saw that some of them had railroad and logging scrip instead of cash. Though it was considered acceptable tender, Gorman thought a man should pay in cash. *That's the American way,* he thought.

Bedal was busy in the front, checking out the dry goods that had just been delivered. "Just need to make sure the count is right," Bedal told the salesman.

Bedal's son, Frenchie, came into the store. "Hi, Papa," he said in French. "Have you opened the new barrel of candy yet?"

Gorman tried not to listen. It irritated him that they were speaking a foreign language in Mansfield, Missouri. *This is America. We should all speak English.*

He winced at the father-son exchange that he couldn't understand. *It ain't too much to ask that if they're gonna live under the Stars and Stripes, that they speak our God-given language.*

Suddenly, Bedal's tone of voice changed. "You should be ashamed of yourself!" Bedal said to his son in French. "Mr. Campbell said you shouted what sounded like a cuss-word at him in French."

"No, no!" Frenchie said to his father in their native tongue. "He kept asking me a question and I just answered, 'Oui, oui.' Is there something wrong with that?"

Bedal tried to explain to his son that in America he should address others in English. But the fact that he was saying this in French upset Sergeant Gorman.

Gorman turned, trying to get away from the foreign language and turned to hear another strange sound. He grimmaced at the Russian that Rabbi Stern and his wife used in the line ahead, gossiping about the day's events.

Why can't they all learn to speak right? Next thing you know, America will be nothin' but another danged foreign country!

Rabbi Stern whispered into his wife's ear in Russian, "I love you."

They must be whisperin' somethin' bad against this country, Gorman thought, his eyes darting wildly around the room to see if anyone else thought as he did.

But what he imagined was the farthest thing from the truth. The Rabbi took a pickle from the barrel next to him and crunched down. He smiled at Gorman, swallowing what he chewed, then said to his wife in Russian. "He is the one who was wounded fighting for his country."

Mrs. Stern nodded her admiration. "Such a brave man. It is a shame that he lost his leg."

The Rabbi looked around at the store's merchandise. "I would never have imagined such riches existed! I wrote my brother that he should come. I told him that I have never regretted one day coming to America."

"You wrote that?" she asked in Russian.

"I said that no man should ever have to bow his head under the yoke of a dictator or czar. That he should come to America. Because here you can be whatever you want and nobody will bother you."

The Rabbi let his eyes wander. He was amazed at the wide array of goods. *There was nothing like this in Russia,* he thought, staring at the nails, wire, stamples, plow points, medicines, foods, clothes, and dozens of colorful bolts of cloth hanging on the walls.

I know they're cuttin' down this country, Gorman thought, sneaking a bitter glance at the Russian couple. His anger was rising, nearing the boiling point.

Trying to control himself, Gorman watched Bedal pull out a long strip of tobacco, and cut off several dime plugs with a hinged tobacco cutter.

"Do you have any Prince Albert pipe tobacco?" Rabbi Stern asked in English.

Bedal nodded, pointing to the box behind him. "New box of one hundred and forty-four twists just came in."

Gorman tried to relax, but his thoughts were driving him crazy. He looked at the meat section, which was mostly salted, cured, and smoked pork, because Bedal didn't have a meat ice box. Slab bacon and side meat, along with some smoked jowl and fatback, were on a table.

But seeing the meat made Gorman hungry so he turned around. He watched one of the back-country farm girls trying on a large, flowered hat. Bedal said in English to no one in particular, "When the new boxes of hats come in, so do the girls."

Gorman didn't smile. He stared at the International Shoe display that had just arrived from St. Louis, but all he saw were immigrants taking over. *Someone's got to stop 'em. Soon there won't be any room left for those of us who were here first.*

He again heard the Rabbi and his wife speaking in Russian and couldn't hold back. "Don't you be sayin' that about my country," Gorman whispered, his head throbbing with pain.

"What . . . what did you say?" asked Rabbi Stern, stammering as he made the awkward switch from Russian to English.

"Nothin'," Gorman muttered. "You wouldn't understand anyhow."

Rabbi Stern shrugged and turned back to speak to his wife in Russian. Gorman made sure he was close enough to the door in case he had to fight his way out. In his fevered mind, he imagined that the immigrants in the room wanted to hurt him.

Where am I? he asked himself. *Is this America or some foreign country?* He adjusted the strap on his wooden right leg, trying to relieve the phantom pains in the toes he no longer had.

Gorman was a loner, a man to be avoided unless you wanted to argue. Though he'd once been just another fun-loving young farmer-to-be in Mansfield, the loss of his leg in the war had changed him.

Two Mexican laborers entered the store and went to the dried beans section. Gorman watched them as they examined the fifty pound bags of beans and rice, speaking in Spanish.

"Why do they charge so much for beans here?" asked the taller of the two men in Spanish.

"Believe me," the other said in rapid Spanish, "this America is no paradise."

"If it is so bad, why don't you go home?" asked the taller man.

"Because there are jobs here!" he said, throwing his hands into the air.

Gorman ground his teeth at the language he didn't understand. He put his hands to his ears, trying to block out the foreign words around him.

Bedal noticed the grimace of pain on Gorman's face and said, "Do you want me to check you out next, Sergeant?"

Gorman cried out, "Doesn't anyone speak English in here?"

The people in the store stopped speaking and stared at the man with the wooden leg. Bedal came from behind the counter. "Sergeant, why don't you come sit down? Have a cold soda. It is my treat," he said in his French-Canadian-accented English.

Gorman looked around, as if he were seeing demons in the air. "This is America! Don't you people know where you are?"

Rabbi Stern reached out to calm him, but Gorman snapped, "I'll slap you bald-headed if you touch me."

Bedal took a step back when he saw the crazed look in Gorman's eyes. Rabbi Stern stepped in front of his wife and then said softly, "Mr. Gorman, do you need to sit down?"

Gorman shook his head, then ducked, hearing the battle sounds again. "Don't you hear it?" he cried out, ducking as another bullet in his mind came at him.

The two Mexicans looked at each other. One made the sign that Gorman must be loco. Rabbi Stern and Bedal moved toward Gorman, who now was beside himself.

"Get back! Get back!" he screamed, dropping the coffee and sugar to push forward his imaginary rifle. "Pick up the colors," Gorman shouted. "Everyone stand tall with the Colonel."

The two Mexican laborers started to laugh, but a look from Bedal silenced them. Gorman backed toward the door, looked around one more time, then pulled it open. Suddenly remembering where he was, Gorman put his hands to his face and said, "This is America. You're supposed to speak English here."

He looked at the Rabbi and screamed, "Don't look at me with those hog eyes of yours." No one in the store said a word until the door slammed behind the soldier.

Finally, Bedal looked at the Rabbi and shrugged. "I guess the bullet took more than his leg."

"He's not riding with four wheels," the Mexican said to his friend in Spanish.

"Crazy Anglo," the other responded.

Rabbi Stern closed his eyes. "Maybe I should go speak with him. Do you agree, Lafayette?"

Bedal shrugged. "I remember when he was a nice young man. He used to have the world by the tail with a downhill pull. But now, he's so mean."

"War will do that," the Rabbi's wife said, shaking her head, then said in Russian to her husband, "That's life. If it isn't chicken, it's feathers."

"I feel sorry for him," Rabbi Stern said in English.

"We all used to," Lafayette said, adding up the groceries on the counter, "until he gave up on himself."

CHAPTER 4

WEDDING BELLS

Rev. Youngun picked up the phone, called the Mansfield Hotel, and asked for Carla Pobst. When she answered the phone, he felt his heart jump and a shiver shoot up his spine.

"Are you sure you have to go back today?"

"Thomas!" she laughed. "You didn't even say hello."

"I'm more concerned with saying good-bye. Why don't you just get one of your friends to pack your things up and stay until the wedding?"

"But we're not getting married until the day after Thanksgiving. And besides, I need to go and close up the house and—"

"And someone else can do it," he said, not wanting her to go. "I hardly slept a wink last night, thinking of saying good-bye to you again."

"But I'll be back before you know it."

"Thanksgiving's almost four months away. That's too long."

"Thomas, you need the time to pack things up. And . . . you've got to tell the kids about the move."

Rev. Youngun sighed. *Telling the kids. That's not going to be easy. They already suspect that Carla and I are getting married, but I don't know how to tell them we're going to move away from Mansfield.*

"Thomas, did you hear me?" Carla asked.

"I was just thinking about what I'm going to say to the kids."

"It won't be easy, but putting it off won't make it any easier."

"I still think I should wait until we're about to go, so they won't have to worry about it."

"You can't put off what you have to do. And you don't want them hearing about it from someone else."

"Who else knows?" Rev. Youngun asked. "Only you and I know and—"

Carla interrupted him. "Small towns have a way of spreading gossip faster than a telegraph line. You've already told the church elders of your plans to transfer to the church in Jacksonville, Florida. One of them could tell his wife and—"

"But they're sworn to secrecy and—"

"And there's never been a secret that a wife couldn't find out. Trust me. And if you don't believe it, wait until we're married. You and I will know everything about each other."

"I guess you're right," he said quietly. "But it will all be worth it once I hear those wedding bells."

"Then I'll be yours forever. Just think about it. A new town, a new church, a new house. Why, it'll be a whole new life for the both of us. It'll be like starting over."

"Let's get married today. Let's go to the justice of the peace and—"

"Thomas! Why, you're—"

"We can honeymoon at the Mansfield Hotel. Just keep that same room you're in and—"

"Thomas, stop this right now! We can't—"

"We could love each other and be together for the rest of our lives."

Carla sighed. "Thomas, the wait will be good for both of us. Absence makes the heart grow fonder, you know."

"Carla, if I wait any longer, the wait is going to about kill me. I'm not some teenager who needs to grow up. I'm a grown man who knows what he wants. And I want *you.*"

"You'll have to wait." She laughed. "And speaking of waiting, if you don't come get me right now, I'm going to miss my train to Cape Girardeau."

After they'd both hung up, Sarah the phone operator unplugged her line. *They're gettin' married and movin' away! That Rev. Youngun is some kind of crazy for that widow. The girls at the sewin' bee ain't gonna believe this!* she thought, plugging in the line and dialing her twenty very best friends.

CHAPTER 5

TEN WAYS

After dropping off Carla at the station, Rev. Youngun decided to go straight home and tell his children about the move. Snapping the reins of the buggy, he watched the lights in his house grow larger.

I'm just going to sit them all down and tell them. Just say we're going to move from Mansfield the day after Thanksgiving. I know they'll cry, but once the tears are over we can all start talking about Florida.

Florida, he thought, shaking his head. *Wonder what that place is like? I've never been out of Missouri. Can't imagine what the ocean must look like.*

With the best of intentions, Rev. Youngun parked the buggy and marched into the house. "Children, come down here to the kitchen." No one answered. "Is anybody here?" he shouted out.

"I'm upstairs, Pa," Terry shouted back.

Guess I'll tell him first. He's probably just sittin' around eating candy. "Do you know where your brother and sister are?" he called out as he walked up the stairs.

"They're outside someplace, Pa."

At the doorway he stopped. "Terry, what are you doing?"

Terry looked up from the paper he was working on. "Just workin' on my writin'."

"Really?" his father said, taken by surprise. "Let's see."

Terry put his hand over the paper. "I haven't finished it."

Rev. Youngun stopped and smiled. "Well, let me know when I can see it."

"I finished all my barn chores, so I thought I'd work on my brain."

Rev. Youngun put his hand to Terry's head. "Are you feelin' all right?"

Terry looked up, puzzled. "Sure, Pa. I feel fine."

"Just checkin'," he said. He watched Terry begin writing again. *I can't tell him now. I've never seen him writing of his own free will. Or happy that he's finished his chores.*

"Where's Larry?" asked Rev. Youngun.

"He's actin' funny," Terry shrugged.

"Funny? What do you mean?"

"Don't know, Pa. Just that he's bothered 'bout somethin'."

"You got any idea what's botherin' him?" asked Rev. Youngun.

Terry thought for a moment. "I think he's worried about boys kissin' girls."

"Kissin' girls!" Rev. Youngun laughed. "Why is he worried about that?"

Terry shook his head. "We saw Cowboy Dan kiss a girl in the movie show and—"

"And what?"

"And I wish he'd kissed his horse, that's all," Terry said.

Rev. Youngun was relieved. *All boys at Larry's age begin worrying about growing up.* "Where's Sherry?"

"Think she's playin' dolls somewhere," Terry said, trying to hide the face he was making at the thought of his sister.

"Why don't you go out and play with her?"

"Play with her?" Terry exclaimed, turning to look at his father.

"Yes, I think you two need to get along better."

"Why?"

"Because you've only got one brother and one sister."

"And that's my tough luck," Terry mumbled to himself.

"What'd you say?" Rev. Youngun asked.

"I said, and that's my good luck."

Rev. Youngun smiled, patting Terry's head. "See, I knew you cared for your sister. Let me know when you want me to read what you've written," he said as he left the room. *I'll tell them all tomorrow. That would be better.*

Terry took his hand off the paper and looked at what he'd written.

10 waYs to get rid of your sester
Bi Terry YounGun

If u want two make yur sester move away, do the folowing:

.1   PuT a spiiider en her hair.
2.   Leeave a deadd mice in her lunch bagg.
3.   Hide a snake inn her bed.
4.   Tie her hair to a waagon weel headin owt of toWn.
4.   Lock her n a trunk and ship her to ChiNNA.
.5   GivE her Up 4 lent.

Terry put his pencil down, his fingers cramped from writing so much. *This is fun,* he thought. *I've already written five ways to get rid of Sherry.*

He counted the ways and came up with six, but the number said five. He recounted and came up with six, then saw the double fours.

Licking the end of his pencil, he began in earnest.

.7   Telll her shez dopted and give her to the ragman.
8.   Put Glu in her undies.
9.   Let a MonSterr take her and tell pA she runned away.

Terry stopped and nodded. *There's got to be a way to sell these ideas. Must be a million other brothers who don't want a sister 'round. Bet I could write a whole book of 'em.*

Needing an energy break, he reached into his hidden candy stash and took out a gumball. Rationalizing that he would need even more energy to finish his piece, he took out two more gumballs and popped them in his mouth.

Got to be one more way, he thought. *What can it be?* An idea came to him, so he began writing.

.10   Put a slimee froG down her Dres.

No, that's not good. He scratched it out and thought of another.

10.   Put a worrM up her nose wheN sheees sleepIN.

No, don't like that. Let's see. Ah . . . this is good.

.10   moVe to nother town and doNt telll her.

I like that! Terry thought, quite satisfied with himself.

Larry came storming into the house. "Pa! Terry didn't help me pitch the hay to the animals."

Terry cringed at the thought of working in the barn but knew what was coming. "Terry," his father called out, "get on out to the barn and help your brother."

CHAPTER 6

KISS-KISS

"What if they have bad breath?" Terry asked his brother. Terry looked at the pile of hay that was his to pitch and shook his head. *If I can just keep him talkin', I'll get him to do my work.*

Larry didn't answer. He was humming to himself as he steadily pitched the hay. Terry shook his head. "If you had a brain, you'd have it in your hand playin' with it."

"What?" Larry asked. "Didn't hear ya."

"I said, what if a girl has bad breath when a boy goes to kiss her?"

Since they'd seen the movie kiss at the Saturday show in town, they'd talked of nothing else when their father wasn't around. Terry thought it was gross and Larry thought . . . well, he was just at the curious age of ten when such things enter your mind.

Larry held a load on the end of his pitchfork. "What's that got to do with anythin'?"

"I mean, how do you kiss a girl if she's got real bad breath?" Terry asked. Without Larry noticing, Terry had been slowly moving his pile of hay onto his brother's pile.

Larry put down his pitchfork. Crab Apple the mule hee-hawed for more hay. "Hold your horses," Larry said, then looked at Terry. "I think the kissin' we saw in the nickel-odeon show was a fake."

"How do you fake a kiss? I saw their lips touch," said Terry.

"I don't think their lips touched," Larry shrugged.

"But I saw 'em on the screen," insisted Terry, moving more hay onto Larry's pile.

"They didn't *kiss*-kiss," Larry said.

"What do you mean, *kiss*-kiss?"

"I mean," Larry said, "that they didn't touch their tongues or nothin'."

"Touch tongues!" Terry said, making a face. "You never told me nothin' 'bout touchin' tongues!" Terry paused for a moment, feeling sick about the whole thing. "You think Pa knows 'bout what you're tellin' me?"

"Suppose he does," Larry said, pitching more hay.

"Why can't you just rub noses like Es-kee-mos?"

"'Cause we're not Eskimos," said Larry.

"Or shake hands or arm wrestle." Terry paused. "But touchin' tongues? That's like eatin' worms." He gagged. "That's like suckin' somebody's face off."

"I can't explain it. It's just somethin' that's supposed to come over you when you kiss."

"The only thing that would come over me would be the feelin' to barf." He spit in disgust. "I ain't never kissin' no one!" exclaimed Terry.

"What about Momma? She used to kiss you," said Larry.

"You put your lips on babies; you don't lick 'em." Terry

thought for a moment. "When Aunt Myrtle kissed you at her house, did you touch your—?"

"Of course not!" snapped Larry. "She's a relative. They only cheek kiss."

"She's got a moustache," Terry frowned. "I hate when she tries to kiss me."

"You never let her," said Larry.

"That's 'cause the one time I did, it felt like a durned porcupine was attackin' me."

"You're such a fibber!" Larry laughed, which gave Terry the chance to push the rest of the hay over.

"Glad I'm finished," Terry said, wiping his brow. "I need a rest," he said, climbing up onto the rail to watch Larry finish *their* work.

Larry looked at the pile of hay. "My pile's grown bigger." He turned and looked at his brother. "How'd you finish so fast?"

Terry leaned back to rest. "While you've been jaw-bonin', I've been busier than a two-tailed cat."

"But I didn't see you fork more than two loads."

"Just learned to work fast and smart," Terry grinned.

"I think you pulled somethin' on me," Larry frowned, throwing another fork full.

"What if you had to kiss 'Asparagus Breath'?" Terry asked, referring to a girl in school who liked to eat cold asparagus for lunch.

"That would be terrible," Larry frowned.

"Yeah, even if you put butter and salt in her mouth, it would be gross." Terry laughed, then shook his head. "I hate asparagus, and I hate the thought of ever havin' to kiss a girl."

Larry stuck the pitchfork in and threw more hay to Crabbie. "Girls like to talk 'bout kissin'," he said.

"Missouri Poole wants to kiss you," Terry teased. "Said she's gonna marry you."

"I ain't gettin' married until I'm Pa's age."

"But she said she wants to get married when she turns twelve, just like her momma did."

Larry leaned against the pitchfork. "There's no way that I'd ever do that. I'd run away from home first."

"I wouldn't let you back in the house if you ever did that," Terry said. "Gettin' married's for the birds."

"Think Pa's really gonna marry Miss Carla?" asked Larry, a look of worry coming onto his face.

"He said they're gettin' hitched," Terry said, shaking his head.

"Pa says he loves her," Larry said.

"He also loves garlic pickles and sardines. Can't believe she's gonna move in with us," Terry frowned. "Our house is too small."

"Pa says it'll be all right."

"House ain't big enough for another girl to be in it," declared Terry. "Sherry's bad enough."

"You didn't mind when Ma was with us."

"Ma was ma. She wasn't a girl," Terry said, getting sad at the thought of his mother and worried that Carla wanted to take her place.

CHAPTER 7

TREMORS

Early that morning, across the country in San Francisco's Chinatown, an elderly woman and her ten-year-old grand-daughter, Yu-Lan, entered the temple. Looking around for an empty space, Grandmother Chan motioned for Yu-Lan to sit behind her.

"Do not disturb those in prayer," Grandmother Chan whispered in Mandarin Chinese.

Clack-clack, clack-clack. The old woman tossed the wooden tiles on the floor in the tradition she had learned as a girl. Her gnarled fingers hesitated before picking up the tiles again. Clouds of scented smoke floated around her head from the incense sticks in her hand.

The murmurs of quiet chants and other *clack-clacking* echoed off the ornate walls and columns of the religious pantheon. This was a wealthy temple, adorned with paint-ings, wood, and stone carvings. Virtually every inch of the room was carved, giving the impression that the entire structure was an artistic creation.

Grandmother Chan sat deep in thought. *There's got to be a way to help him.* She was barely aware of the others in the chamber. She was only concerned with helping her grandson, Tong.

Beside her was a couple praying to have children. Next to them was a very sick man, lying on the stairs, praying for good health. Reverent visitors behind them visited the portals around the room, praying for help. An elderly man held an unrolled scroll of Chinese calligraphy letters he had written.

Grandmother Chan took a quick glance at the brush-and-ink letters. She raised her nose, judging the man to be of bad character by the sample of his calligraphy.

He uses bad tools. His brushes are not made from fox hair. He's probably using simple rabbit hair. She turned back to her tiles, then glanced again at his brushstrokes. *The tiger character is not big and bold enough. It does not reflect the character of the animal.*

Grandmother Chan looked at the wooden tiles and frowned. She picked them up. *Clack-clack, clack-clack.* She dropped them again.

Something is wrong, she thought, tossing the wooden pieces on the stone floor. *The animals have been nervous all day,* she thought, raising her ear to the dogs barking and the horses baying.

Yu-Lan knelt quietly behind her grandmother. She looked at the man holding the scroll, trying to remember what her Grandmother had taught her about the Four Treasures of the Scholar's Studio. *Brush, ink, inkstone, and paper, that is what she said.*

Yu-Lan had noticed the face her grandmother had made at the man's work. *She has judged him to be of bad character.*

Even if he falls down and calls for help, she will ignore him because of the quality of his calligraphy.

Yu-Lan's ears were perked to the various Chinese dialects being spoken in the room. *The temple is always crowded,* she thought. *Day or night, festival or bad times, people always come to ask questions, make offerings.*

Although Yu-Lan's grandmother still attended this temple, Yu-Lan's father had brought her up in the Chinese Methodist Episcopal Church. Nevertheless, Yu-Lan felt drawn to the beautiful, serene room. It was a place where Chinese people came to rest, eat, talk with friends, and watch other people. It was also a place to escape from the anti-Chinese fears that were sweeping through California and the nation.

Yu-Lan looked around the room, trying not to be obvious in watching what was going on. She looked at the carved and painted walls, columns, and tiled roof that seemed to link the temple together as though it were one, large Chinese story.

She recognized the subjects from the old stories she'd learned at home. *The Romance of the Three Kingdoms. The Legend of Deification. The Story of the Tang Dynasty.*

Yu-Lan tried to read the intricate calligraphy tales of the ancient Chinese heroes, but found herself concentrating on the colorful dragons overhead. *They look as if they could fly off the ceiling and eat the painted flowers on the walls.*

Yu-Lan was fascinated by the old ways of her grandmother. *What would Grandmother say if she knew that I listened to her Chinese but thought in English?*

Yu-Lan had never told her Grandmother about her thoughts being in English. It was just something the older woman wouldn't understand. Even though her grandmother spoke English, she preferred to speak in Chinese as a sign of respect to the old ways.

Yu-Lan had smiled when Grandmother stood her in front of the temple and said, "Look around. The courtyards here are open to the sky. The temple is open to the public. But what you believe is private."

Yu-Lan knew that the old woman had come to pray for help for Yu-Lan's seven-year-old cousin, Tong Shu-Jen. *Father says that Tong is retarded. He said Tong will not live to reach old age.* She thought of the flattish skull and facial features of her cousin and said a hopeful prayer.

For a moment she was sad, then Yu-Lan watched a young couple sharing a bowl of rice in a nearby portal. Grandmother Chan turned around.

"Yu-Lan, quit staring. It is most impolite. You're making me and the other visitors nervous," Grandmother Chan whispered.

Before Yu-Lan could respond, Grandmother Chan was back with her wooden *bei,* hitting the stones. The aging lady looked at the statue. She was lost in thought. She shook her head, then continued. *Clack-clack, clack-clack.* She paused, looked, then hit them again. *Clack-clack, clack-clack.*

The polished wooden face of the ancient statue in front of her grandmother stared back at Yu-Lan. For a moment she thought the lips moved. Yu-Lan turned from the piercing stone eyes, feeling a shiver run down her back.

It was just the incense smoke, she decided. *It makes everything seem to move.*

I wish I were out playing jackstones, she sighed, thinking of the game the Korean girls had taught her. She smiled, remembering the turnip lanterns and the bamboo paper wad guns that they'd also shown her. *Or flying a kite! Now that would be wonderful,* she nodded, thinking of the colorful kite her father had made her.

I love the freedom a kite has in the air. Floating above everyone, everything. Floating above the world where no one can hate you . . . hate you because you're Chinese.

A feeling that someone was watching came over her. Goosebumps raised on her thin arms. Yu-Lan looked again at the embroidered robes on the bearded statue and its subordinates.

She gulped and stared. *The eyebrow moved!* She looked again through the clouds of incense that had darkened the faces of the statues in the room. *No, it was just the smoke . . . that's all.*

Taking her eyes off the symbolic birds and flowers that graced the walls beside them, Yu-Lan turned. "What are you thinking?" she asked her grandmother, wishing they could leave and go play in the park as Grandmother had promised.

"Something is wrong." Grandmother Chan frowned, eyeing the pieces of wood again. She found herself unable to concentrate and didn't know why.

Yu-Lan again heard the sounds of horses baying and dogs barking. Two dogs ran into the temple barking madly. They were chased out by the temple keeper with his large straw broom. "Grandmother," said Yu-Lan, "the animals are very nervous outside."

Grandmother Chan squinted her eyes and listened to the sounds of frightened animals from all around the temple. "The goats and pigs are squealing." Grandmother Chan nodded. "Something is wrong."

Yu-Lan suddenly felt nervous. "We should go."

Grandmother picked up the wooden *bei.* "Not yet. I am not finished."

"But—" Yu-Lan said, feeling a slight shake of the building.

"But nothing! You will do as I say," she said. Bowing to the statue, covered by a cloud of incense from the burning sticks in her hand, Grandmother Chan raised the sticks up and down, then dropped them. *Clack-clack, clack-clack.*

A tremor shook the building and the statues. Some people got up and left quickly. Yu-Lan tugged at the black sleeve of her grandmother's long robe. "Please, Grandmother. We should leave."

Grandmother Chan thought, reaching for the wooden *bei. Confucius says that a wise man looks for what is within, the fool for what is outside. I am looking within. Why can't I see the answer?*

Suddenly, a massive earthquake rocked the building, knocking Grandmother Chan over. Yu-Lan fell by her side, covering her from the painted tiles that fell around her.

The frightened sounds of the animals were overtaken by the screams of fear from people in the streets outside. Yu-Lan and her grandmother tried to stand, but another tremor knocked them over.

The old lady looked around. *What is going on?* she thought. *The earth is moving. I've got to get Yu-Lan home.*

With determination, Grandmother Chan rose to her knees. Yu-Lan winced at the sound of her creaking joints. Picking up the *bei,* Grandmother Chan hit them. *Clack-clack, clack-clack.* Clouds of aromatic smoke wafted around her. She closed her eyes, thinking of Tong. She wished the affliction could be taken away from him.

"Come, Grandmother. We must go home now," Yu-Lan said urgently, looking around. They were the only ones left in the temple.

"Silence!" Grandmother reprimanded, watching the pieces of wood fall. She watched, then smiled. Grandmother Chan bowed, touching her head to the cool flagstone four times.

Yu-Lan knew that their visit was finally over.

Grandmother Chan got to her feet and silently took Yu-Lan's hand.

The temple jolted again violently, knocking them against the ornate walls. "It is time to go!" Grandmother Chan shouted, pulling Yu-Lan along as she crawled through the immense red-framed doorway at the front of the temple.

As they stumbled outside, the ground split before them. Buildings began to crumble. The whole world seemed to be coming apart. San Francisco was falling down. A great earthquake was destroying their world.

All Yu-Lan could think of was an old nursery rhyme she'd been taught. *All the king's horses and all the king's men* . . . she looked at two buildings fall . . . *couldn't put San Francisco together again.*

It was all they could do to crawl, but Grandmother Chan pulled Yu-Lan forward. "We must get home before the world opens up and eats us."

CHAPTER 8

EARTHQUAKE

Grandmother Chan and Yu-Lan had crawled until their knees were raw, then took refuge in the doorway of a building that still stood. The tremors had stopped, but they clung together, feeling helpless and lost. Their whole world seemed turned upside down.

Horses ran loose down the street, blind with fear, trampling anyone in their way. Injured people in shock were walking, screaming, and crying all around them.

Chinatown was ablaze. Like a tinderbox, the wooden homes stacked one on top of the other, were in flames. The sky was blackened with the smoke of a thousand homes burning out of control. A scared Chinese family huddled under the roof of a stone building across the street that hadn't fallen yet.

Yu-Lan felt the ground lightly shake. "We must get home. Mother and Father will be worried about us."

"Speak in Chinese," her grandmother snapped.

"Why?"

"Because you are Chinese." The old woman wished she hadn't dropped her *bei*. "I don't know where we are,"

Grandmother Chan said, trying to find a familiar landmark. "Everything . . . all the street signs are gone," she said, looking around bewildered.

Yu-Lan knew that if they didn't keep going they'd never get home. "It's this way," Yu-Lan said, tugging at her grandmother's arm.

"But we're safe here," Grandmother Chan said, pulling her back.

A hard aftershock jolted them yet again. The partial building left standing across from them, crashed down on the family who had hidden there from the stampeding horses.

"We must get into the open," Yu-Lan screamed. "This building will fall too!"

The old woman tried to protest, but Yu-Lan pulled her as hard as she could. They'd managed to crawl only ten feet, when another aftershock hit, crumbling the building under which they'd just stood.

"Help, help!" shouted an anguished man.

Yu-Lan looked around. There were bodies scattered down the street. People were moaning, some crawling with broken legs. A woman ran by carrying a dead child in her arms.

"Help . . . help me!" the man shouted again. Yu-Lan looked, but couldn't find where it was coming from.

The old woman came back to her senses. *There are too many to help. It is either us or them. I hope Tong is being watched,* she thought, thinking of her retarded grandson.

"Come on," Grandmother Chan said, "we can do nothing for them all."

"But I heard someone—"

"You heard the moans of ghosts and ancestors, which is

what we will be if we don't get home. Your father will know what to do," Grandmother Chan said.

Yu-Lan looked over at the building which had collapsed in front of her. A dirty arm was reaching out from under the rubble. "Help," came the shaky voice of the arm.

"He's trapped!" Yu-Lan shouted, rushing over before her grandmother could stop her.

"Come back, Yu-Lan!"

Yu-Lan looked at the marble slab. The fingers were making tracks in the earth. "Are you all right?" she asked, looking hesitantly under the slab.

She saw the face of a white man staring back at him. "My legs are caught. . . . I think they're crushed."

Grandmother bent down next to Yu-Lan to look under the slab. "May the gods and your ancestors have mercy on you," she said to the man. Straightening up, she looked at Yu-Lan. "Let's go," she said in Chinese, trying to pull her away.

"But he's trapped! We must help him," Yu-Lan pleaded.

Grandmother Chan shook her head. "There is nothing we can do."

"That's not right!" Yu-Lan screamed.

"Help me. Don't leave me!" the man shouted out.

Reacting from her heart, Yu-Lan reached under the rock to help the man. "Take my hand. I'll try to pull you out," she said in English.

The hurt man grasped Yu-Lan's hand and struggled forward. Yu-Lan felt like retching when she heard the man's leg bone crack.

The man screamed and let go of Yu-Lan's hand. "Leave him be," the old lady said. "You cannot change the will of the gods!"

Yu-Lan bent down again to help, but was knocked on her face by another aftershock. Her grandmother fell on top of her. All they could do was try and hold onto the bucking ground. It was like being on the deck of a ship. Grandmother Chan felt as if she were again in the hold of a small ship rocking in the storm off the China coast.

Yu-Lan watched in horror as the slab slowly slid down, crushing the life out of the man below. "He's dead, Grandmother," Yu-Lan said, tears in her eyes.

When the shaking stopped, the old lady stood up, dusting herself off. "See? I told you that you can't change the will of the gods."

"But he asked for our help," Yu-Lan whispered.

"Look around," Grandmother Chan said sternly. Yu-Lan looked at the death and misery surrounding them. "These are your own people and you can't help them. We have to wait until the earth gods have stopped being angry before we can get back in their favor by helping others."

"But, Grandmother—"

"But nothing. Come on. We have to go home," Grandmother Chan said.

As they made their way in the direction they thought was home, Yu-Lan and her grandmother gripped hands tightly. It was as if they were alone at the end of the world.

Another tremor knocked them down. As they held onto the ground, they heard chanting behind them. Grandmother Chan turned to see one of the temple priests walking toward them through the rubble, swinging his incense burner from side to side.

"It is the blind one," Grandmother Chan whispered to Yu-Lan.

They watched in quiet astonishment as the priest with the vacant eyes walked past them.

Grandmother Chan shook her head. "You better pray to your god right now."

"I am," Yu-Lan whispered.

"Good," Grandmother said. "I don't want to go to my dead ancestors just yet. I'm still mad at my late uncle."

The old woman and her granddaughter moved on. Stepping over bodies. Not looking at the wailing children. Avoiding the crushed and crawling animals who hadn't been graced with death yet. The magnitude of the suffering numbed them.

After a few more blocks, the dead became just numbers. Like so much rubble. Yu-Lan realized that she could do nothing to save the people trapped under the collapsed buildings they passed by.

A set of *bei* lay beside a dead Chinese man. Grandmother Chan asked the gods for forgiveness and put them in her pocket. A few steps further was another dead man with a pistol in his hand. Grandmother Chan looked at the pistol.

"Come on, Grandmother," Yu-Lan called out from a few yards down the street.

"I'm coming," Grandmother Chan answered. She walked over and picked up the handgun and stuck it under her robe. Though she had never touched a firearm before, she knew that it was something one of her sons might need in the future.

Firewagons and Red Cross vehicles fended through the ruble in the distance, going in every direction except toward Chinatown. That the Chinese were treated differently was a fact of life for Grandmother Chan. For Yu-Lan, it was something that she just could not understand. And as a Chinese Methodist Episcopal, she knew that racial hatred was sinful.

The great San Francisco earthquake of 1906 destroyed everything Yu-Lan and her family knew and loved. Everything that they called home in a land thousands of miles away from China, where Grandmother Chan and Yu-Lan's parents had been born.

At the edge of what had been the street they lived on, the earth had cracked open. "Where is Father?" Yu-Lan whispered, but Grandmother had already seen him.

Yu-Lan's father, Shih Chan, knelt on the other side of the street, almost hidden by the smoke from the burning building behind him. He was wailing with sorrow. Praying as he had been taught by the Methodist missionaries, beseeching God for help.

"Look! It's Father," Yu-Lan said. She waved her arms. "Father! Father! We're here!" Yu-Lan shouted, jumping up and down and running down the street toward him.

Grandmother Chan looked down through a clearing in the smoke and saw Yu-Lan's mother lying in the center of the cracked earth, twisted and torn like a rag doll. She couldn't be alive.

"Come to me," said Grandmother Chan, grabbing Yu-Lan and squeezing her close.

"What . . . what is it?" Yu-Lan asked.

Shih Chan looked over at his mother, his eyes swollen with tears. Grandmother Chan bowed to her son, acknowledging his loss.

"She is gone . . . gone!" Shih cried out.

Grandmother Chan just nodded, her heart aching for the pain of her son.

"Please, Grandmother. Why is Father crying?" Yu-Lan asked, breaking loose from her grasp.

In the moment it took to look, the ground shook and the crack in the earth closed, sealing forever her mother under the ground and searing the image in Yu-Lan's mind forever. Yu-Lan screamed.

Why, God, why? Yu-Lan cried through her tears.

Grandmother Chan took Yu-Lan in her arms. Her eyes misted. *What have my son and my granddaughter done to deserve this?* The old woman wanted to think about something, anything, but not about the anguish her son felt.

The pistol poked in her side and she shifted uncomfortably. *Guns are bad,* she thought, but didn't want to think about that either.

The sound of her son's sorrow made her eyes well up. The weight of his grief flooded over her. *Please give me strength,* she beseeched her gods. *Make him understand that death is but part of the natural cycle.*

CHAPTER 9

FEELINGS

Laura's stomach felt sick. *Must be something I ate,* she thought, standing in the bathroom near their bedroom in Apple Hill Farm. A moment before she had been sitting on the bed, talking with Manly, and the next thing she knew, she felt sick.

"Think you got the flu?" Manly asked from the doorway.

"Don't know . . . maybe it was that fish we had for dinner last night."

"I don't feel a thing," Manly shrugged.

"You've got an iron stomach," Laura said, then holding her hand over her mouth as the feeling came up again.

Manly walked quietly to her side and put his hands on her shoulders to steady her. "Do what you have to do. I'll help you," he said.

Laura did feel better after it came out of her. Manly helped her to the bed. "You want some of my ma's stomachache cure?"

"What's that?" she asked weakly.

"Just put three drops of turpentine on sugar and swallow

it slowly." Laura started to gag at the thought. "Maybe I should just get you some hot tea."

Fifteen minutes later, Manly brought her up a cup of hot tea and the newspaper. "Here, drink this. I'll go back down and get you some soft bread."

"Thank you, Manly," she said, sitting back against the pillows. She closed her eyes, listening to the familiar sound of his staggered walk.

When he came back up, Laura was smiling. "You look like the picture of health," he laughed. "Are you sure you're not faking it?"

"I don't know what came over me," she said, shaking her head. "But I've had a queasy stomach lately and—"

"I think you've just been workin' too hard. You need to quit doin' so much writing and just relax. Let me do the worrying."

Laura sipped the tea and looked at the paper while Manly opened the windows. "Remember the group sings we used to go to when we were courtin'?" Manly asked. Laura nodded. "Those were fun times, sittin' round that old piano down at the church."

Manly took a deep breath from the opened window. "You remember that time we were at a sing and you girls were makin' popcorn and candy?"

"Yes, Manly," she said. It was a story that Manly liked to tell.

"Me and the boys were out havin' ourselves a good-ole cob fight when Johnny Johnson beaned Billy Boxley on the head. He took off like a bat out of you-know-where, and caught his pants on a nail jumpin' over the fence. He ripped his britches clean off!"

Manly laughed until his eyes watered. "That was a barrel of fun," he smiled. "Let me know if there's anythin' else I can get you."

Laura nodded again, her eyes focused on an ad. She looked at the picture of the new car and grinned. "Look at this," she smiled. "This is what I want."

"What's that?" he asked, walking over to the bed. He looked at the picture.

"That," she said, "is a 1906 brand spanking new Cadillac. That's what I want."

Manly frowned. "Come on, Laura. Your Oldsmobile's not but a year old. You can't be buyin' a new car every year."

"Why not? I like the looks of that one."

"Heck," he said, "we probably don't have more than nine hundred miles on the one in the barn." He paused. "I'll tell you one thing."

"What's that?" said Laura, eyeing the car in the ad.

"I'm glad they didn't have automobiles when we were courtin'."

"Why's that?" she asked, looking up.

"'Cause courtin' in a buggy's better. We were never in a hurry, and when we got to smoochin', the horses always knew the way home," he winked, raising his eyebrows up and down. "If you get my meanin'."

"I get your meaning," she said, then paused, shaking her head. "What a tragedy."

"Now what?" he laughed. "Did they sell the last Cadillac?"

"No," she said. "Look at this!"

San Francisco Earthquake Kills Thousands!

San Francisco, California—Miles of flames are reducing most of the city of San Francisco to ashes tonight, the day after a severe earthquake jolted the entire Bay area. Military officials estimate that more than ten thousand people may have been burned to death or crushed by falling debris.

Whole sections of the town have been wiped out, including the wharf district, Chinatown, and Nob Hill. Red Cross efforts are under way to help. Donations of cash, food, and blankets are desperately needed.

Manly whistled. "Glad we're not out there."

Laura closed her eyes at the horror for a few moments, then looked at Manly. "My heart goes out to those people."

"Nothin' we can do about it from here," he said, interrupting her reading.

"What did you say?" asked Laura.

"Those people in San Francisco are in the hands of God and the U.S. Government. Ain't no four better hands in the world to help them through that earthquake," he smiled as he got up and stretched.

Laura stood up and pulled her robe tight. "You're right. I'll just say a prayer, then start this day again," she said, looking at the window. "It's going to be a wonderful day."

"Wonderful?" he asked, watching his wife dance a jig around the room. "Just a moment ago you got sick, and now you're sayin' it's a wonderful day?"

"I've just got a feeling that something good is about to happen, that's all," she smiled, then gasped. "I wonder if he knows?"

"He, who are you talkin' 'bout?" Manly asked.

"Chan. About the earthquake. Chan has relatives in San Francisco."

"Give him a call," Manly said.

Laura went to the kitchen and rang up her Chinese friend. "Mr. Chan, this is Laura and—"

"You are still going to play Mah-Jongg with me today?"

"Yes, but—"

"Good. I look forward to our lessons, and today is our day."

"Mr. Chan. I was calling to see if you'd read the paper today."

"I have it here, but I haven't read it yet. Is there something I should read?"

Laura paused, not knowing how to break the news. "There's been a terrible earthquake in San Francisco, and I know you have relatives there and . . ." Laura paused. There was nothing but silence on the line.

"Mr. Chan, did you hear me?"

"I heard you," he answered. Laura could hear the sound of paper rustling over the phone. "I have the paper opened here and . . ." He paused, mumbling something in Chinese.

Laura closed her eyes, sad for what he was going through. "I don't understand what you're saying," she said quietly.

"This is terrible . . . so many people hurt . . . I have to contact my relatives and—"

"Go to the train station and send a telegraph message. That's the fastest way."

Manly said from the pantry, "Bet all the lines are down."

Laura then said, "If you can't get through to San Francisco, send a telegraph to the California Red Cross in Sacramento. They'll have a list of the . . ." Laura stopped.

"Of the dead," Chan said quietly.

"But the chances are that they're alive and well, Mr. Chan," Laura said. "If you want, I'll get Summers to send a telegraph message to the newspaper out there. That would probably be the fastest way."

"I would be forever in your debt if you would do that for me."

"Consider it done, Mr. Chan," Laura smiled.

"I will pray for them," Chan said.

"So will I," said Laura. "I guess we should cancel our lesson."

"No. Please come," he said. "And bring me the news that you find out."

"I will," Laura promised. She put down the phone, then rang up Summers and made the request.

"Glory be, Laura! How are we s'posed to find Chan's relatives? Must be a couple hundred thousand Chinese folk in San Francisco!"

"Just try for me, Andrew. Call up Chan and get the spellings of their names. Then ask for someone to check them against the list of known dead."

Summers coughed. "Like I got nothin' better to do."

"I'll owe you a favor."

"Please, don't go overboard with gratitude."

"Thanks, Andrew," Laura smiled, hanging up.

Laura felt her head, then felt her stomach. *I wish I had some peaches. A jar of peach halves in thick, sweet syrup would taste mighty good.*

Manly walked into the kitchen. "Look what I found," he smiled, holding up a dusty jar of Georgia peaches.

CHAPTER 10

DIFFERENT

Yu-Lan stood by her father and grandmother. Ashes floating in the air from the fires that still raged in parts of San Francisco mixed with her tears. Black streaks squiggled down her cheeks.

The funeral for her mother seemed out of place since all of Chinatown seemed dead. Though San Francisco was working to crawl out of the rubble, Chinatown was not on the priority list of places for the city to help.

The ceremonial elegance and ritual of the event, with the few friends who had survived and cousins from the next street over, stood in stark contrast to the cinders and rubble around them. "Your mother's in a better place," the minister said quietly, patting Yu-Lan's head.

"I hope so," Yu-Lan whispered, clutching the doll that her mother had made her as a gift.

"You have to believe," the minister nodded.

"I'm trying," she said, tears running down her cheeks.

"I'm sure she is in heaven," the minister said.

The minister turned to talk with her father. Yu-Lan looked around the Chinese cemetery, then over toward the white cemetery. She clutched her Chinese Bible tightly, hoping that her mother was in a better place. She tried to understand this invisible line in death that was in stark contrast to the color lines drawn in life.

There's only one heaven . . . a heaven for all of us. Dead Chinese people here and dead white people there. We are kept from schools and have to live in Chinatown. Yet we all go to one heaven. That doesn't make sense.

She thought of the white missionaries who had died in the Chinese War to bring them the new religion from the West and the Chinese Bibles, like the one she held. Then she thought of how the white people in San Francisco seemed to hate them because they were Chinese. It was all very confusing to the young girl.

Her father, Shih Chan, looked down at the casket at the bottom of the grave. He tried to listen to the minister, but knew that the words did not describe his wife.

Not one word describes her smile, her laughter, the baby we had together. The sparkle in her eyes. Her sacrifices for her family. That is what should be said.

Shih looked around. His heart ached for his wife and the pain of his daughter. *My wife is gone. Our house is destroyed. My mother said it's the anger of the gods . . . because I became a Christian. She says the gods are not happy and won't be unless I go to the temple and consult them.*

Shih looked at his mother. "Come *clack-clack* with me," she'd told him over and over, showing him the new pair of *bei* she'd found. He had to admire the resourcefulness of his mother. Even in the midst of the disaster, her black robe was pressed and clean. Her hair was in place. Her nails were trimmed. It was her way of saying that she would survive.

Then he smiled. The smile was out of place, an involuntary reaction to the sadness around him, but he couldn't help it. He looked at his mother and shook his head, thinking about the harmonica she'd learned to play.

I just hope she doesn't start playing her harmonica now. It is so unChinese of her the way she plays. She sounds like the minstrel show players I heard at the wharf.

His worry about the past and future was the reason for the mixed funeral. Shih had decided to ask their minister and his mother's temple priest to say prayers.

The white-robed Chinese Methodist Episcopal minister read from the Bible, while the black-robed temple priest swung incense in one hand and tinkled a bell in the other. Candlesticks were stuck in a circle on the ground and plates of food were placed in the center. A whole cooked pig sat beside the priest, who chanted in his high-pitched voice.

Yu-Lan watched, confused. Her mother had converted to her father's church; yet the funeral was a mixture of the new and the old ways. *Father said it was in deference to Grandmother,* she thought, looking up at the handsome old woman who had managed to find her jeweled hair clip in the ruins of their home and wear it.

Grandmother Chan nodded to the priest. Two temple assistants stood beside him. One slowly beat a small drum and the other clashed two cymbals at the correct points in the priest's prayers.

The minister closed his Bible and walked up to Shih. "So much death within our small church," he said. "I am sorry your wife is gone. But she has gone to be with God."

Shih nodded. "Thank you for coming."

"It is all I have done for three days. Sixty people in our

church and I have said burial prayers for thirty of them." He looked at Yu-Lan and patted her head. "You will have to be strong . . . to help your father and grandmother."

Yu-Lan nodded, feeling numb.

"Will you rebuild?" the minister asked Shih.

"I don't know."

Shih's half-brother Leu Shu-Jen, and his wife Ko, came forward to offer their condolences. They also were Chinese Methodists Episcopals. Their seven-year-old son, Tong, the retarded child who worried Grandmother Chan so, stood behind them. He nodded at Yu-Lan, who was his special friend.

"Part of our house survived," Leu said. "You, Mother, and Yu-Lan must come live with us."

Shih looked at his brother and bowed his thanks. "I would not want to burden you. You have always had more than your share," he nodded. They both knew he was referring to Tong, who smiled up at him.

The minister patted Tong on the head. "It is always the children who suffer," he said, looking into Leu and Ko's eyes. "No one should say that the tragedy of children like Tong are part of God's plan for creation."

Grandmother Chan kept her tongue. *That is so callous. Their God should love all his people.*

Leu spoke up in Tong's defense. "Tong is not a tragedy. Good or bad, he is part of God's good creation. He, like us, has a divine purpose. Otherwise, it would be as when rich people saying that those who do not have the blessings they have are less in favor with God."

"Gift from . . ." Tong stammered.

They all turned. "What is he saying?" the minister asked.

"Gi . . . gi . . . gi . . ." Tong stopped, frustrated.

Yu-Lan helped him. "He's saying gift from God. In Sunday school they've been trying to teach him to say he's a gift from God. That he's special. But he has trouble remembering."

Leu shook his head. "The doctors told me that, though his head is big, he'll never be able to memorize things."

His wife Ko frowned. "Tong is different, but he can learn."

Grandmother Chan took Tong in her arms. The temple priest began chanting loudly, drowning out their conversation. The drum beat increased and the cymbals clashed.

"But I insist you come stay with us. We are family," Leu said into his brother's ear.

"You are most kind," Shih said, "but we have pitched a tent where our house stood and—"

Ko took his hand. "You cannot stay here. It is not good for your daughter."

Grandmother Chan interrupted her, "I have already told my stubborn son that. The gods and ancestors do not want him to grieve. They want him to come back and believe again."

Shih shook his head. "Yes, yes . . . you have told me that many times today already." He turned to his brother. "I will stay here for seven days, and then we will come to your house until I can figure out what to do."

Tong began wandering off toward a collapsed house, and his parents jumped to pull him back.

Yu-Lan took her father's arm. "Where will we go, Father?"

"I don't know. If we stay here, we have to stay in Chinatown."

Yu-Lan looked around. "But it is all destroyed. Why can't we go to the hills and build a home?"

Leu burned with anger over the memory of abuse he suffered since coming to America. "Because Chinese are restricted to Chinatown. This is the only place it is safe for us to live."

"But why?" Yu-Lan asked. She knew that the newspapers and community did not like the Chinese coming to America, but she didn't understand it.

"Because we look different," Leu said.

Grandmother Chan looked at her sons. "This is hard for a young girl to understand."

"It is time she learned," Leu said. "And it is something I wish he could understand," he said, looking at his son, Tong, who just smiled.

"I know about it," Yu-Lan said, "but I don't understand it."

"The white devils hate us," Leu said bitterly.

Ko took her husband's arm. "You're scaring Yu-Lan and Tong," she said. The young boy's face was buried in his mother's dress.

"We Chinese have to learn not to be so afraid!" Leu snapped.

Grandmother Chan shook her head. "We are all afraid of something."

After the funeral, Yu-Lan helped her father load what belongings they had salvaged into baskets. Grandmother Chan sat on what was left of a chair, softly playing her harmonica.

"I wish we could move from here," Yu-Lan said. "I wish we could live in a place where Chinese would be welcome."

Shih put his arms around his daughter. "I received a telegram from cousin Chan in a place called Missouri. Read it," he said, handing it to his daughter. "He calls Missouri the 'land of promise'."

"Are there a lot of Chinese there?" Yu-Lan asked, after reading it.

"He wrote last winter that they are the only Chinese family, but he says the town treats them with respect."

"Where is Missouri?" Yu-Lan asked.

"It is in the middle of America," Shih said. "Cousin Wang Chan says that it is a place where people still spend hours sewing their own clothes and spend all day making dinner for their families."

"But we do that here," Yu-Lan said.

Shih thought for a moment. "But in this Mansfield, it is a different life. Cousin Wang wrote that people stop and talk to him. He has friends . . . neighbors . . . white neighbors."

"White neighbors?" Yu-Lan asked in astonishment. "They don't make him live in Chinatown?"

"There is no Chinatown in Mansfield," Shih said. "There is just one town . . . and it is for everyone."

Yu-Lan thought for a moment, then asked, "Is it farther away than China? Grandmother says we should leave here and go home," she whispered, looking over at the old woman who was lost in her music.

"Home?" Shih smiled. "You were born in America. This is your home. In China, you would be a foreigner because you speak English and have different ways."

"But we're Chinese and—"

Shih put his finger to his daughter's lips. "America is a land that we came to. To have a chance to eat and—"

Leu came over. "Mother, it is time to leave." The old

woman played one last, long note, then put the harmonica back into her pocket.

"Come on," Shih said, taking his daughter's hand. "We have to get our things."

Leu picked up Tong and carried him down the street with his wife, Ko, following closely behind. When they were a block away, Leu said to his brother, "There is a group of Chinese going to Vancouver, British Columbia, in Canada."

"Canada?" Shih asked. "Why Canada?"

"There's a big Chinatown there with lots of jobs."

"I have telegraphed cousin Wang Chan in Missouri about coming to visit. He's the one who—"

"Yes, yes, I know. The cousin who's made a fortune in the golden mountain."

"Yes, he says Missouri is the promised land and that the Chinese are welcome there."

"Let's discuss it this evening," Leu said, walking to catch up with his wife.

As Yu-Lan and her father walked along carrying their baskets, Yu-Lan asked, "But I still don't understand why they don't like us."

"I told you. It's because we're different," her father said.

"But everyone's different. Everyone looks different to me."

"But not everyone's Chinese," her father said. "That is the difference."

For the next two days, relief efforts from all over the country formed to send food, clothing, and money to aid the thousands of destitute and homeless in San Francisco. It was money sent from the heart to help fellow Americans. But the Chinese were left to fend for themselves.

They were Americans, but they looked different.

CHAPTER 11

PARTY LINE

Small towns have an invisible communication system not found in big cities, and Mansfield was no exception. Phones were still a brand-new thing, and the county telephone lines —party lines—with ten to fifteen neighbors hooked onto each one, was the fastest way to spread any kind of news.

Every time the phone rang, it rang in everyone's home on the line. Everyone heard the ring and everyone listened. It was a combination of noisiness, curiosity, and concern.

If someone was sick, most considered it their obligation to help out and, miraculously, food and whatever else was needed would appear on the doorstep of the family in need by the next morning.

Which was how Sherry learned that her father was planning to sell the house and move from Mansfield. Sarah, the phone operator, told it to several neighbors who began to gossip about who'd be buying the Younguns' house.

Sherry, who liked to listen in on the party line every chance she could, heard them talking. Sarah said, "And imagine, Rev. Youngun sellin' that house, gettin' married, and movin' with a new wife and three kids to Florida."

Emma Lou whistled. "He must be crazy doin' all that at once. If it were me, why I'd wait a year or two 'fore I moved, to let things settle."

Then there was a sobbing on the line that neither woman could account for. "Is that you, Emma?" Sarah asked.

"Ain't me," Emma Lou answered, trying to identify the sound. "Sounds like a little girl."

"Who's listenin' on this line?" Sarah asked loudly.

Then they heard the click, followed by the static silence on the line.

"I guess they hung up," Emma said.

Sarah sighed. "Wish people wouldn't listen in on the line. Sometimes they hear things they ought not to hear."

Sherry sat in the kitchen, tears streaming down her face. Rev. Youngun walked in humming, thinking about Carla.

"Sherry, what's wrong?" Sherry just shook her head. "Come on, tell Pa what's wrong," he said, kneeling down beside her in the chair.

"Don't want to go," she blubbered.

"Don't want to what?" he asked, but he knew. He knew she'd heard about the move. *How did she find out so soon? I should have told her. It should have come from me.*

"Oh, sweet thing, your daddy wanted to wait until the last minute to tell you about the wonderful adventure we're goin' to have. Why, when we get to Jacksonville, I'll show you—"

Sherry pushed away from him and ran from the room crying.

"Hey, Pa, what's wrong with Sherry?" Larry asked, walking into the kitchen.

"Something's on her mind," Rev. Youngun said glumly.

"I'll go talk to her," Larry said.

"Let her go," he said, watching her run from the window. "She needs to be by herself."

He turned to Larry. "Go get Terry. There's something I want to tell you boys."

While Rev. Youngun broke the sad news to her brothers, Sherry ran across the field. She wanted to run forever. Sherry's feet just moved by themselves because her mind was so upset.

Don't wanna move . . . don't wanna leave . . . my friends . . . my pets . . . ain't fair . . . ain't fair.

Sherry ran through the briars, cutting her arms and face. *I feel like dyin' . . . don't wanna live if I can't live here.*

She thought about her piggie Little Bessie, about Crab Apple the mule, about T.R. the turkey, about Bashful the fainting goat, about Beezer the parrot.

I won't leave my pets. They love me. I'll stay with them. An idea began to gel. *I can live in the barn. Go to school by myself. Maybe Larry will stay with me. Maybe even*—she thought about Terry, then shook her head. *He better go with Pa.*

Bumping head-on into a branch, she fell to the ground, crying. A lump began to grow on her forehead, which throbbed with pain.

The only person she could run to was where her feet were going. She was going by instinct. Running to the man who was always there to help. A man whom she'd never see again.

I gotta get to Mr. Springer. He'll let me stay with him. I can be his daughter. He won't move away.

Sherry ran across the ridge and down the hill to Maurice's farm. She saw him sitting on the back steps, drinking a glass of something.

"Mr. Springer! Mr. Springer!" she cried out, as she flew down the hill.

"Sherry? Is that you, girl?"

She didn't answer. Her heart was beating so fast. Her head throbbed and her feet moved in a blur.

Maurice stood up and walked toward her. "What's wrong? Somethin' happened, baby?"

Sherry flew into his arms, sobbing as if it were the end of the world.

"There, there, baby," he said quietly. "You can tell ol' Maurice all about it." But she was crying too hard to speak, so he just waited for her to calm down, just smoothing her hair.

After a few minutes, she took a couple of deep breaths and snuggled her sniffing nose against his shoulder. "Pa's takin' us away," she whispered.

"You goin' on a vacation?" he asked, smiling. Sherry just sobbed. "Can't be that bad. Talk to me, girl. Ain't nothin' so bad that ol' Maurice can't handle it."

"Don't wanna go," she whispered. "Don't wanna leave you. I love you, Mr. Springer."

"Leave me? How long you gonna be gone?"

Sherry looked into his eyes. "Forever," she whispered.

"Forever?"

"Don't want Pa to sell the house and move us away and—"

"Hold it, girl. What you talkin' 'bout? Sell the house . . . move? You just talkin' nonsense," Maurice said, trying to look confident but feeling a burst of concern shoot up his spine. He'd heard speculations but hadn't thought anything about them.

"I heard the ladies talkin' on the phone. Pa's gettin' married and sellin' the house. Gonna move us away to the Floor."

"The where?" Maurice asked, his mind a jumble.

"To Floor . . . Flori-i-da," she whimpered. "That's what they said."

"Florida!" Maurice exclaimed. "That's a million miles from nowhere."

"I love you, Mr. Springer," Sherry whimpered.

"I love you, baby. You know ol' Maurice loves you more than life itself," he said, squeezing her to help hold back the tears that dripped down his own cheeks.

"Can I live with you?" she whispered. "I'll be a good girl. I'll be your daughter . . . yours and Eulla Mae's."

"That'd be wonderful, baby," Maurice said, "but your daddy loves and needs you."

"But I don't want to leave you," she said.

"And I don't want you to go." He lifted her so she could look into his eyes. "Listen," he said. "Just 'cause you're gonna move away, don't mean you're gonna be totally gone from here."

Sherry gave him a puzzled look, wiping away her tears.

"That's right." He smiled, blinking his eyes, wishing he could rub them. "Put your ear right here," he said, touching on his shirt, over his heart.

Sherry put her ear on his chest. "What do you hear?" he asked softly.

"I hear your heart beatin'," she answered.

"That's good. You just keep on a listenin'. 'Cause in every beat of my heart, you can hear your name bein' called."

He lifted her up. "Now, let me put my ear to yours," he

said, listening to the beat of her tiny heart. "Yup, ah-huh, I can hear it callin' my name."

He listened for a moment longer, then began to walk her back to her house. "With every beat of my heart, I'll be thinkin' of you. And with every beat of your heart, you can think of me. That way we'll always be together, even when you move away."

"But I want to *stay* with you," she whispered.

"Can't. Wish you could but you can't. So we'll just have to live together between the beats of our heart."

Sherry worked her tiny fingers into his big, gnarled hand. "Please, can I stay and live with you?" she begged.

Maurice just shook his head no, staring at the little hand in his. "Can I listen to your heart again?" she asked.

"Certainly, child," he said, glad that her head was turned away so she wouldn't see him cry.

Thump-thump, thump-thump, thump-thump. Sherry listened to her name being called out. The sound of his beating heart soothed her mind and as she closed her eyes, falling asleep, the sound of the heart changed to, *Sher-ry, Sher-ry, Sher-ry, Sher-ry, Sher-ry.*

CHAPTER 12

PLEASE STAY

Maurice carried Sherry back to her house, then sat on the steps waiting for Rev. Youngun to come out from his study. Though the sun was shining, it seemed to Maurice that the whole world was covered with gloom.

There won't be no sunshine when they're gone, he thought. *I was planin' to take 'em campin'. Show 'em how to cook on a campfire and really fish.*

He thought back on the adventures they'd had. How they'd won the horse race on their mule. And how he'd saved them when they were lost on Christmas Eve in the blizzard.

And the football game! he laughed out loud, tears rimming his eyes. *When them kids wore the pots on their heads 'cause we couldn't afford no helmets. They looked so funny that they* had *to win the game!*

For a moment he was bathed in happy thoughts. *And teachin' them 'bout right and wrong . . . Why, I've been there when they needed me. Who's gonna help these fool kids if I'm not around?*

He remembered the trip to the dog show in St. Louis, when they had stuck with him when the hotel wouldn't let a black man stay there. *Those kids shinnied down a sheet rope and came with me. Went to a juke joint, we did,* he laughed, thinking how they'd kept the secret from Rev. Youngun.

And that dog show! he laughed to himself. *Alice Roosevelt herself was there and these kids saved her dog. Man-oh-man, was that some trip! And it was only two months back when they got that mule to move with the dill pickles.*

Maurice laughed until his sides hurt, then rubbed his hands over his eyes. The realization of the enjoyment, laughter, and love that he had with the Younguns, and what it meant to his life, suddenly washed over him.

"Maurice, is something wrong?" Rev. Youngun asked as he came out onto the porch. Maurice slowly took his hands off his face and nodded.

Rev. Youngun walked down the short steps and sat beside Maurice. "You look upset," he said, concerned. "What happened?"

"Don't want you to go," he said quietly. "You don't got to move."

Rev. Youngun took a deep breath. He had planned to wait until the wedding to announce that they were moving. "Who told you?" he asked quietly.

"Sherry came running over. She told me."

Rev. Youngun shook his head. "She must have been listening on the party line again." Maurice nodded. "I shouldn't have put off tellin' them."

"Have you told the boys?" Maurice asked.

"I just told them."

"How'd they take it?"

Rev. Youngun shook his head. "Larry's taking it the worst,

but he'll survive. We all will. You will," he said, looking fondly at his friend.

"Is your decision final?" asked Maurice.

Rev. Youngun sat on the steps beside Maurice. "I don't know what to do. Carla wants me to get another house so we can start fresh without the memories of the past and—"

"And that's foolish talk. A house is what you make of it," Maurice said earnestly.

"And a house is how you feel about it," Rev. Youngun said quietly.

"Don't you feel good 'bout your house? It's a nice house."

"I like the old place. The kids are comfortable. We've got good neighbors," Rev. Youngun said, putting his hand on Maurice's shoulders, "and I like the town."

"Then why are you movin' away? Can't you just get another place somewhere else 'round here?"

"It's not that simple," Rev. Youngun sighed.

"Heck, if it's money you're worried 'bout, I'll give you some of my land to build on."

"That's generous of you, Maurice but—"

"But nothin'!" he said, standing up and facing his friend. "You won't have to pay me a thing. I got an extra five acres alongside Apple Hill that you can have free and clear. I'll even help you clear the land and build the house. Everyone in the county will come have a house-raisin' party. Please stay. Will ya?"

Rev. Youngun put his hands over his face and took a deep breath. Then he looked at his friend. "If it was just another house, why, I'd love to live on your land and pay you for it. But the Methodist council has asked me to consider moving and—"

"And what about the church you built?" Maurice exclaimed. "It's got your sweet spirit inside it."

"Built from scratch." Rev. Youngun nodded. "I remember when I first started preaching here. There weren't anymore than a dozen folks showing up. Now we're almost running out of space."

He thought back to the beginning of the church as if it were the beginning of life itself. How they'd first held services in people's living rooms and at brush arbor meetings in the shade of the frame and bough put up for the day. Then they had enough people and enough money to build a church. Rev. Youngun saw the church in his mind, remembering who had done what as the structure went up.

"Then that's more than enough reason to stay," said Maurice. "Your congregation needs you."

"My church has grown and borne fruit, that I will admit," Rev. Youngun said.

"Fruit! Heck you got the whole tree here. You can't go!"

"Sometimes you can't do what you want to do."

"Does gettin' married mean you got to move?" asked Maurice.

"No, gettin' married is something I want to do. Movin' is something I don't want to do."

"Then why do you got to go?"

"'Cause the council wants me to go. They've got a church in Jacksonville that they want me to take over."

"But Florida? That's halfway across the country. Might as well be halfway to the moon."

"That's where they're sending me," said Rev. Youngun.

"Just don't go," Maurice said, brightening at the idea.

"Don't go? What would I do?"

"You can come farm with me. I'll build you a house, and the kids can learn how to be farmers, and you and Carla can raise another houseful of kids and—"

Rev. Youngun took his friend by the arm. "Maurice . . . Maurice," he said gently. "I'm a man of the cloth, a man of God. That's what I do. That's what I *want* to do."

"But what about the kids? They don't want to go!"

"I think this is the way God planned our lives. That we each have a cross to bear and this pain of leaving might be yours and mine."

"Might be your cross," Maurice said, putting on his hat and turning to go, "but it shouldn't be mine. Ain't no sense puttin' yourself and others through misery over a woman. That's what it's all about, ain't it?"

"Some of it, but not all of it."

"I knew it," he said, kicking the dirt. "You could tell the council you don't want to leave, but you don't want to tell that woman that you're not gonna move. That's it, right?"

"I don't know," Rev. Youngun sighed, shaking his head. "All I know is that I love Carla Pobst with all my heart and soul, with the very breath of life inside me. And that I want everything to work between us." He paused and looked into Maurice's eyes. "You've got to understand, Maurice. I have a second chance at life. I don't want to lose it."

"That chance don't do me much good," Maurice said. "But it *is* your life, and you got a right to feel what you feel. But so do I. Just 'cause you want to leave don't mean that anyone else wants you or the kids to leave."

"They love you, Maurice." Rev. Youngun nodded.

"And I love them. You don't know how much I'll miss 'em," he said, turning away so that Rev. Youngun wouldn't see the tears in his eyes.

"You've been good to them. They love you, Maurice," Rev. Youngun repeated softly. "That's somethin' no one can ever take away from you."

"They're like my own children," Maurice mumbled, watching the breeze blow the grass slightly. "Like my own children."

"It'll hurt for a while," said Rev. Youngun, "but you'll get over it."

"Some words are easier said than livin' through." Maurice stood up and slowly walked back toward his house with a hopeless, sinking feeling. *I wish I hadn't heard about it until they'd moved. Now every day is gonna be as long as a month of Sundays.*

But Rev. Youngun's eyes were moist also. He was thinking about his children and his church. Remembering how the first year they'd paid him just nine dollars, and part of that was a four-dollar hog.

The only question they'd asked him when he applied for the job was, "Do you have two living wives?" When he said no, they hired him for life . . . or as long as he wanted to stay.

In the back of his mind, he remembered the first service, when they had a dozen people and one hymnbook they all shared. As the book and rhythm stick were passed around, each person sang loudly, waving the stick in the air to keep the beat.

The building seemed to echo that first hymn they sang:

> O praise the lord, sing to the Lord a new song.
> Sing His praise in the assembly of the faithful

And in the front row of that service, quiet as church mice, were his three children, proud of their father and the church he had built. Standing beside them was Norma, looking at him with all the love in the world in her eyes.

"Do you have two living wives?" he heard them asking as he remembered the vision of his late wife.

Two living wives . . . no. But I've got one I gave my first heart to who will always be alive in my mind, he thought, and began weeping the tears of transition. He was going to remarry. He was moving away to start again. *Maurice and everyone else will just have to understand.*

CHAPTER 13

MAD FOR MAH-JONGG

Chan focused on the Mah-Jongg board. His clacking of the playing tiles was getting on Laura's nerves, but it was the only way he could keep from thinking about the earthquake.

"Mr. Chan," she said, "I can't concentrate."

Chan looked up. "Sorry. I'm just nervous."

"Do you want to send another telegram?"

Chan pondered for a moment, then shook his head. "I'm sure that my message will get through."

"At least Andrew Summers learned that your relatives aren't on the list of the dead."

"But the list is not complete."

Laura saw the worry in his eyes. "I've been saying prayers for your relatives."

"So have I," Chan nodded. "Now, let's continue to play," he said, wanting to keep his worry and grief private.

"Okay, Mr. Chan." Laura smiled and looked back at the board.

"You don't have to call me Mr. Chan. You can call me Wang."

Laura smiled. "I've just always called you Mr. Chan, that's all."

"It makes me feel like such an elder." Chan began clacking his tiles again. "Ah-hah! I think I just put together a . . ." he smiled and shouted, "Mah-Jongg!"

"You win again," she laughed, wondering when she was ever going to master this Chinese game.

"It just takes time." He bowed to her. "Some people spend a lifetime trying to master it."

"That doesn't give me much confidence," said Laura.

"Do you want to play another game?"

Laura looked at the ivory tiles with bamboo backs. "It reminds me of other games, but I just can't seem to get the hang of it."

"Don't think of any other game when you play Mah-Jongg," he smiled. "Just pick your tiles, set them on your rack, and create the magical combination."

"That's just it," Laura said. "Sometimes you have to make a combination of the numbers and sometimes a combination of the images shown."

"Such confusion," Chan said. "Perhaps if we played for money as we did in China, you would learn faster."

"Why faster?"

"Because he who learns fastest doesn't go broke first," he said, trying to suppress a grin.

"You know, Mr. Chan," Laura said with a smile, "you never seem to get angry."

Chan bowed slightly, then said, "It is because I believe in *ren-ching-wie.*"

"Ren what?" asked Laura.

"*Ren-ching-wie* . . . in English it means the flavor of

human feeling." He paused to see if she understood. "It is a flavor as ancient as China itself, but as fresh as this morning flower here," he smiled, nodding to the blossoms in the water bowl.

"I'm trying to understand," she shrugged.

Chan nodded. "It is hard for Westerners to understand, but for us Chinese, it goes back thousands of years to the time of Confucius, who taught us that human considerations come first."

He paused, trying to see if she understood. "That feelings are as important as facts. Americans live by the rule of law and logic, but the Chinese believe it is the human flavor—*ren-ching-wei*—which has made Chinese society and customs so resilient."

Stephen Scales, the telegraph operator at the train station, came through the door. "Got a message for you, Mr. Chan," he said, putting down his sack.

"A telegram?" Chan said. "From where?"

"Got it right here," Scales said, handing it to Chan.

Chan looked at it. "It is from San Francisco," he said, hesitating to open it. Scales said good-bye.

"Aren't you going to open it?" Laura asked.

Chan's hands were shaking. "I have been so worried about my cousins. So many people died and—"

Laura picked up her purse. "I think I'll leave you to read your letter in quiet. Dr. George ought to be back now."

"No, that was rude of me," Chan said. "Please stay and have some tea," he invited, his hands shaking.

"I'll see you next week when we continue our Mah-Jongg lessons," Laura said gently. She closed the door quietly behind her.

Chan pulled down the shades. He held the message in his trembling hands, worried about what it would say.

Finally, gaining courage, he opened the envelope and slowly read it.

To: Wang Chan, Mansfield, Missouri
From: Shih Chan, San Francisco, California

Dear Cousin Wang, the tragedy of the earthquake sent many of our friends and family to their ancestors. My wife died and was buried properly today. We have lost our home and live with a second cousin. You told me Missouri is the land of promise. May we visit? My daughter and mother would be no burden. Leu Shu-Jen and his wife and special son would like to visit also. Though we are Chinese Methodist Episcopals, we are not treated here like humans. We want to find a place where being Chinese will not bring us more misery. With respect and regards, Shih Chan.

Chan put the letter down. *Mansfield has treated my family with respect because we have proven ourselves. But would they have respected us if there had been more than one Chinese family?*

The wall behind the counter caught his eye. He looked at the photographs of his wife and son and the only one he had of his parents. It was like looking at lost years that had to account for something in his mind, but now he didn't know what to think.

He thought about his son, Li Sung, who seemed to be forgetting the old ways. *Would he act so American if he had relatives around? Would he respect the old ways more if he saw how proper Chinese acted?*

Chan had come to learn that in this land of immigrants,

little things can change moods and tempers in a flash. Mansfield was his land of opportunity. He didn't want anything to change that. It was Chan's dilemma. A dilemma of family responsibility versus the reality of America, of life in the golden mountain.

Inside the envelope was a clipping, which Chan unfolded.

ASIAN CHILDREN BARRED FROM PUBLIC SCHOOLS!

The Mayor of San Francisco promised to keep Asian children segregated from whites in the public schools. In a move commended by the publisher of the Hearst newspaper chain, who has warned about the Yellow Peril that is threatening America, the mayor took the first steps to ensure that the Chinese are kept segregated.

Chan didn't bother to read the rest. Attached to the clipping was a picture from the newspaper. It showed two Chinese boys having their heads shaved.

He hung his head in shame. Chan had tried not to think of the Asian Exclusion Leagues that had formed along the West Coast and were spreading east. He had kept quiet about the Chinese Exclusion Act of 1882, which had been reaffirmed in 1892 and in 1902, when the Senate vowed to permanently exclude Chinese people from entering America.

I just want to live quietly, not be troubled. What happens out there is not my concern.

The door opened with a creak. Chan turned and saw Larry and Terry Youngun stick their heads in. "Can Li come out to play?" Larry asked.

"He's not here," Mr. Chan smiled.

"If you see him," said Terry, "tell him we're tryin' to get up a game of baseball."

Chan watched the two boys run off down the street. *Life is good in the golden Ozark mountains,* he thought.

CHAPTER 14

GOLDEN MOUNTAIN

Chan sat in the dark, keeping his tears private. His cousin's letter brought back memories he didn't want to think about.

With a sigh, he reached under the counter and took out his photograph book. Carefully wiping the dust off the cover, he opened it and paused. A picture of his late mother and father sat before him.

He breathed deeply and a fragrance from one of his herb bottles in the front counter triggered a memory. A memory of a mountain, South Mountain just outside of Chungking, a world away in China.

On the facing page was a picture of him and his sister. *We played paper ball that morning,* Chan thought, remembering how he and his sister were the only children on their rural property. *I thought we owned the world,* he smiled, knowing now that his father was only a tenant farmer for the landlord.

His father had come in that morning and announced that they would have their pictures taken and then they would leave their farm. The children had never been farther away than Chungking, so going anywhere sounded like an adventure.

"We are we going, Father?" Chan remembered asking. *I was just fourteen and full of curiosity.* Chan smiled.

"We are going to America!" his father announced proudly, then danced around. He grabbed his children's hands and danced with them in a circle.

"And what is this?" his mother had asked, coming into their simple one-room home.

"We received the tickets. We are going to the golden mountain," he laughed.

"But it is so far away," his wife whispered.

"When we get to the golden mountain, all our problems will be over. We will be landowners in America," his father had boasted to the family.

Chan closed his eyes, remembering his father's words: "Here, everything costs a lot because we have nothing. But in America, if we are thrifty and work hard, we will build our own future."

So the Chan family joined the millions from around the world who came to America for economic reasons. The golden mountain was like a magnet, as America drew to its shores the hard workers and dreamers of the world.

But getting there was not easy. Chan bowed his head at the memory of the trip by boat to San Francisco. Two hundred Chinese crowded together in the bottom bunks of the boat.

It was hot; it stank. Chan frowned, not wanting to think about the fetid conditions that caused so much pain. *Mother couldn't stand the food. When she got the fever, there was not enough clean water. No clean sheets. She needed fresh air, but they wouldn't let us on the decks. They thought we were just coolies. "Chinese coolies, more railroad workers," the seaman had jeered.*

The memory of his mother's high fever and their futile efforts to save her sent a shudder of agony again through Chan's body. A tear came to his eyes as he thought about her burial at sea.

We were allowed on the top deck to watch her body drop into the sea. We watched her disappear, wrapped in a simple silk shroud. My father wanted to pray in the old way for my mother, but the captain of the boat wouldn't let him.

"I don't want any of you heathen Chinese sayin' none of your celestial prayers on my boat. This is a God-blessed, God-fearin' boat. You understand?"

My father nodded and whispered to my sister and me in Chinese, "Pray to the gods and ancestors for forgiveness. Ask them to lift her from the sea and take her back to South Mountain."

My father embodied grace. He would not let the captain get to him.

At the funeral, my sister rubbed her eyes so hard that she scratched one red. "Don't do that," *my father had scolded.* "They won't let red eyes into America."

The next morning, her eye got worse, and all the other Chinese began whispering that she had the red eye. "What are we going to do?" *Father moaned. He had lost Mother and now faced a strange land with two children to raise.*

Chan thought he heard rain pattering on the roof, but wasn't sure. He paced slowly around the store, thinking of his arrival in America.

The doctor at the entrance center in San Francisco ex-

amined my father's eyes and then mine. My sister clung to me, her left eye hidden. I had told her to peer out with her good eye, as if she were scared.

My father gave the signal, and she started crying on cue. "What is wrong with your sister?" the doctor asked.

In broken English, my father said, "She is sad for her mother."

My sister began rubbing her eyes, bawling loudly.

"Tell her to be quiet," the doctor said. "She's disturbing everyone."

"Can we go through?" Father asked.

The doctor looked briefly at their faces, then waved them through. "Okay, everyone in this family has good eyes. Next?" he called out.

"We made it to the golden mountain!" Father said, crying as he set foot as a free man in America. "The golden mountain is where we will make our home."

He never even complained about the racial insults, Chan thought. All he cared about was getting to the golden mountain.

The golden mountain, Chan thought, shaking his head. America was everything we wanted it to be in our minds. A place where you could work for yourself, not be a slave to the landlord. A place where the harder you worked, the more you earned. A country formed by people of all races.

Chan shook his head and sighed at the naiveté of their thoughts. Of the people, by the people, for the people. Chan had learned the difference between words and reality. Between thoughts and deeds. Between in-church and out-of-church.

I have done well here, he sighed. America is a mixt

many colors, but it is a strange mixture. Chan felt the rain in the air. *You start with white paint, you mix in black, red, and yellow, and you end up with white.*

Chan paused. *I have learned that all good things take time. Maybe we have not stirred the paint pot hard enough. Maybe we have allowed our happiness of being in the golden mountain to sink us to the bottom of the paint pot.*

Raindrops drummed on his tin roof. He walked over and parted the curtains, looking out at the summer shower. The hot, humid August air misted for a moment, then cleared, leaving a rainbow hanging in the air over the Ozarks.

I've never seen a rainbow with a white band on top, he frowned. *But that is what America seems like to all who fill its rainbow of colors.*

CHAPTER 15

BODY TALK

Laura got to Dr. George's office, just as he was coming back from an all-night house call. He put the gunny sack full of cabbage that he'd accepted as payment onto the floor. He took off his coat.

"When I took this job, they told me that the country would produce a livin' for me if I'd just let it," he said. "Bet I take in as much food and such as I do cash." He wiped his brow. "A man last week paid me with a cord of wood. Mrs. Adams paid me with a dressed chicken yesterday. And for helpin' a family last night, they paid me in cabbage," he laughed. "Just glad I like sauerkraut."

"You look tired," Laura said.

"You would be too if you'd slept on an itchy sack of straw ticking last night."

Laura smiled. "What happened?"

"Had to make a backwoods call. Some country boy came over late, said his momma's baby was ill. So like I always do, I got my bag and tried to start my car, but the engine wouldn't turn over."

"So how'd you get there?"

"Had to use my old horses, Topsy and Turvy, and go in the buggy. Took a while, followin' behind the boy on horseback, but then when I thought we were about half-lost up near Mountain Grove, he stopped at a creek, and pointed to a skiff sittin' on the bank."

Dr. George paused. "Said to go 'bout a half-mile down creek and there'd be a man waitin' with a lantern."

Laura listened quietly, always amazed at his dedication. Dr. George continued. "Found that lantern and then went to a one-room shack and found a baby with spinal meningitis. Had to wrap the little thing up in some old muslin, and rested him on a dirty pillow while we rowed back to the buggy. I got him up to Mountain Grove and woke up the pharmacist and got some medicine into the child."

"Is the baby going to live?" Laura asked.

"God willin', I think so," Dr. George sighed, rubbing his legs.

"Did you hurt yourself?"

"Naw, just got a charley horse wadin' in that cold water. My legs drew up in knots last night and my feet still ache." He sighed, rubbing his leg hard one last time. "Now, let's see what's ailin' you."

Laura sat patiently while Dr. George examined her. "I've just not been feeling well lately, Doc."

Dr. George listened to her heart. "You say you've not had much appetite?"

Laura nodded. "But I still feel bloated and have gained some weight. And then with being sick lately, I just think I've come down with something. Think it's consumption?"

Dr. George prodded, listened and felt her back, chest, and

stomach, then sat back and smiled. "Sometimes the hot August air can do this," he grinned.

"Never had it before," she said.

"And sometimes you can feel this way from overeating or getting a bit of the fever," he smiled.

Laura was impatient. "I don't see what's so funny!" she snapped. "I'm not feeling well and you're smiling."

Dr. George chuckled at her anger. "And sometimes this comes from things in the springtime."

He paused. Laura waited for him to say something else. Finally, she couldn't bear it and spoke first. "What things in the springtime? What are you talking about?"

"Oh, could be any one of several things," he said, picking up his notepad. He raised it in front of his face to hide his grin, then turned and paced as if he were seriously studying it. "Let me read you a list of things, and you tell me if any of them apply to you."

Laura nodded.

"During the springtime, did you eat right?"

"Yes." She nodded.

"Did you sleep right?"

"Far as I can remember."

"Let's see, did you get plenty of walking in?"

"I guess so? What's all this got to do with my feeling sick?"

"I'm gettin' to it. You've just forgotten a few things," Dr. George said. "Let me refresh your memory a bit. Did you travel much?"

Laura thought for a moment, then nodded. "I went to St. Louis twice."

"And the purpose of those visits?" Dr. George asked, suddenly sounding very formal.

"Well, I went two months back to meet with the women suffragists. Oh, and I went with Manly on a belated . . ." Laura stopped then whispered the last word, ". . . Honeymoon."

"That's it!" Dr. George laughed loudly. "That's the cause of your not feelin' well!"

Laura knew what he was saying but had to ask. "Do you mean I'm . . ."

"Yes. That's what I mean. Laura Ingalls Wilder, at the grand old age of thirty-nine, you're going to have a . . ."

". . . baby," she said in unison with him.

"That's right, a baby. What do you think about that?" Dr. George smiled.

"I don't know," she said, feeling dizzy from the news. "I'm almost forty years old. Isn't that too old?"

Dr. George shook his head. "I don't think you got anything to worry 'bout."

"What am I going to tell Manly?" she wondered aloud, looking out the window.

"Tell him he's a daddy. He's goin' to have another baby around Apple Hill Farm," Dr. George said, his smile returning.

"A baby," she smiled, patting her stomach.

Dr. George stood up and stuck his thumbs in his suspenders. "There's gonna be the patter of little feet around your house come the New Year. Yes sir, soon it's gonna be cigar-handin'-out time!"

"Cigars?" said Laura, putting her hand to her mouth.

"Not for you!" Dr. George laughed. "You got to take care of yourself. You're eatin' for two now!"

"I feel sick," she said, thinking about the smell of cigar smoke.

"That's just your body talkin' common sense to you."

"What?" she said, feeling queasy.

"When you're pregnant, your body talks to you. It tells you what it needs and what it doesn't want around. It's protectin' that little baby inside you."

Laura put her hands to her stomach. *Life,* she thought. *There's new life inside me. What in heaven's name am I going to name her?*

CHAPTER 16

CRAZY TALK

Manly thumbed through a copy of *Police Gazette*. From the corner of his eye, he watched Billy Pickle and John McAlister giving haircuts.

"I'll just take a bit off the top and take the sides down, okay?" Pickle asked the man under the towel. It was the same question he'd asked the last two customers while Manly waited. It was the same question he asked everyone who sat in his chair.

Wonder why he asks anything? Manly shrugged, turning another page.

"Next?" McAlister called out, lifting the towel off his latest victim.

Manly slumped down in the chair.

"Next?" McAlister called out.

Lafeyette Bedal leaned over to Manly. "I think you're next?" Bedal smiled.

"No, I'm sure you're next," Manly said hopefully.

McAlister looked at the two of them. "Which one of you guys is next?"

Manly was glad that Billy Pickle had given McAlister a job,

but that didn't mean he would be glad to have McAlister cut his hair. He just felt uncomfortable around anyone who didn't know his left from his right and held a straight razor behind someone's head.

"Lafayette, it's your turn. You got here before Manly," McAlister said.

"Rats," whispered Bedal to Manly. "You got all the luck today."

Manly sighed. Neither man wanted to hurt McAlister's feelings but it was common knowledge to all the men around town—except for Pickle and McAlister—that at the barber shop, luck of the draw could indeed be dangerous. Not only did almost every one of McAlister's customers leave with some nick or scrape, they all left with haircuts looking like they'd been attacked by a hay-mowing machine.

Knowing he was safe this time, Manly sniffed the bay rum wafting through the air, looked at the mystery tonic bottles on the wall, and couldn't suppress a grin at Bedal's discomfort.

"How you want it cut?" McAlister asked.

"Just cut the hair, don't cut me," Bedal said.

"That's an order," Pickle said to his number-two barber in the two-man shop. "I don't have any more bandages."

"Bandages?" Bedal asked, sitting up.

"Yup," Manly teased. "A man yesterday needed two hundred and forty-eight stitches."

Bedal began to take off the towel. "I think I see someone trying to get into my store. I'll come back later."

Manly laughed. "We were just joshin' you. Sit back down."

Bedal sat back and tried to relax, but couldn't. It was all he

could do to sit in the chair while McAlister sharpened his razor on an old suspender that hung from the chair.

Manly stopped turning the pages. "The Heathen Chinese" article caught his eye in the magazine. He began to read, hoping that his friend Mr. Chan never saw it because it blamed Chinese people for everything bad that had ever happened to California and America.

Manly stopped reading. *This is wrong! Whoever wrote this just hates the Chinese,* he thought, shaking his head. Manly knew Mr. Chan and considered him a fine person and a friend.

Manly flipped through the other stories in the publication, shaking his head. "Hoodlums Make Life Miserable for the Coolies," "No Bullets Wasted on the Heathen Chinese," "Every Citizen Turns Against the Chinese." It made Manly sick.

"That's just a bunch of horse droppin's, ain't it?" asked Jimmy "Harmonica" Preston.

Manly looked up at the black man who was sweeping the hair from around McAlister's chair. "Worse than that," Manly said as he put down the *Gazette.*

"You and Blindman ended your fallin' out?" Manly asked. It was known in Mansfield that Blindman Thomas and Harmonica Preston feuded constantly as to who was the best player in the Ozarks.

"That old fool still won't accept the fact that I'm the best," Harmonica said, pushing the broom along.

"He still plays good," Manly said.

"But I play better and my time's come to be harp king of the hill."

"Next?" Pickle called out. Manly stood up.

"You finished with that magazine?" Sergeant Gorman asked.

Manly looked at the war veteran with the wooden leg, and nodded. Gorman had a flash temper and was one person with whom Manly generally avoided conversation. "You can have it, Sergeant. It's just a crock."

Gorman took the magazine. "This is the issue I've been waiting for. All 'bout what the patriots have done in other towns to drive out the Chinese." He opened the magazine and showed Manly a picture of cowboys in Arizona harassing a Chinese man. "Manly, this is what we should be doing in Missouri, don't you think?"

"The war's over, Sergeant," Manly said.

"Wars never end. There's always a last battle somewhere," Gorman muttered.

"In your mind," Harmonica said, pushing the broom by.

"What'd you say?" asked Gorman with a snarl on his face.

"He said, in due time," Manly said, winking at Preston.

"I agree," Gorman nodded.

"Next," Pickle called out. Manly limped over and stepped up into the chair. "How you want your hair cut, Manly?" Pickle asked.

"Oh, just a trim."

"Just a little bit off the top and take the sides down?"

"Right," Manly shrugged.

"Okeedokey," Pickle said, putting his comb and scissors to Manly's head. "Saw your wife go into Dr. George's. Anythin' wrong?"

"Nope," Manly said. "She's not been feelin' well. Just goin' to have the Doc check her."

CHAPTER 17

PITTER-PATTER

On the ridge above the house, Laura sat on her thinking rock, trying to come to grips with the news that she was pregnant.

I wonder what Manly will say? she thought, then frowned. *I hope he'll be happy.*

Laura shook her head, thinking about the pitter-patter of little feet around Apple Hill Farm. *Not much he can say now, is there?*

She thought about his age, about his limp, and got a worried, sick feeling in her stomach. *But he's almost fifty years old. This won't be easy news to swallow. But he's always wanted a son and . . . what will Rose think?* she wondered, thinking about her daughter, who was away visiting relatives before entering college.

A drive will do me good, she thought. She got her purse and hat and went to get the Oldsmobile from the barn. Laura took the back roads, winding over the ridge tops. The endless variety of trees in the wooded hills soothed her nerves. The high meadows and meandering valleys seemed to frame the beautiful, almost mystic, foggy horizons ahead.

The bushes and fences were covered by the wild bittersweet vine that was like the people of the Ozarks. It survived on the thin, rocky soil just like the people who had struggled in these parts for a hundred years to survive.

It had been a while since Laura had been down these roads. She drove through Whippoorwill Valley and remembered the night she and Manly stopped and kissed on the spur of the moment. *The moon was out. Rose was away at school. The whippoorwills were calling all around us. Our hearts were beating together. We felt like teenagers again.*

On a whim, she took some back roads she'd never been on. She waved to a farmer tending to his dairy herd of holsteins, jerseys, and guernsey cows. His wife was working a small garden. A crashed automobile, pirated for parts, rusted alongside the barn. Laura wasn't sure of the roads ahead, so she stopped and called out to the farmer, "Is this the way back to Mansfield?"

The old man, hitched up his overalls and trudged over. "What you in such a rush for?"

"I'm not in a rush," she said. "I'm just not sure of the way."

"Lady," the farmer smiled, "tomorrow ain't gonna be no different from today, so no use hurryin' along in your fancy automobile."

Laura grinned. "I just need to get back home to Mansfield. If you'd be so kind as to—"

"There's only one way," he lisped through his missing front teeth. "Just keep goin' straight and you can't miss it."

His wife walked over, carrying a bucket of water with a ladle in her hand. "Want a cool-off drink?"

Laura, feeling the heat from the drive, nodded. The cool

water was what she needed. "Looks like your garden is coming along fine," Laura said, dabbing her lip with her hanky.

With a smile that showed more feeling than teeth, the old woman said, "We'll have enough preserves this year to last through the winter. My tomatoes, beans, and peas've already took good root."

She paused and looked at Laura. "You got the glow."

"The what?" Laura said.

"The glow. You're with child, ain't ya?" Laura blushed and nodded. "Well, you best start walkin' so the birth will be easier. Women today have a harder time birthin' 'cause they don't walk as much."

"Thank you for telling me," said Laura.

"And another thing, don't eat a lot of beans." Laura looked perplexed, and the old woman nodded. "Yup, that's right. Too many dried beans will give you a hardheaded baby. And another thing: Keep a good thought in your head every day."

"A good thought?"

"You listen to me," the old woman said, leaning up to Laura. "You got a big influence on that baby growin' in your belly. The mind is developing right along with the body. So if you want a child that works hard and ain't a lazy bum, you best keep busy and keep your mind on the good of life. Don't think about anythin' that's contrary."

Her piercing stare set Laura back. "Thank you for telling me."

"Do what I say and you won't have a tough time trainin' the little one. 'Cause it's already instilled in his little mind."

From behind her came the sound of a clanking old wagon. "Hey, Hobart," the old man called out. "What you got new today?"

Hobart Klemmedson, a lifelong mountain peddler, pulled his wagon full of wares to a stop. "Got some good pie pins, two for a nickel," the old peddler said, looking behind him, "and some seed, fertilizer, and fresh eggs that I got in a trade from McSpadden back over the hills yonder."

Laura left the old friends to haggle and headed back on the road toward Mansfield. *People in the Ozarks don't have life easy, but they have a good life. They work at it,* she thought. *They thrive on being away from the city life. The hills and woods are their buffer. The separation requires self-reliance. They're like the bittersweet vine.*

Laura crossed a shallow stream that ran over a dip in the road and emerged down a steep, winding grade. The trees closed in around her as the road got narrower. A wild turkey dashed across the road in front of her and a deer stood by the road, watching her pass.

She grinned at him as she drove along. At the edge of a high meadow, Laura stopped to stretch her legs.

Spinning around, feeling giddy at the beauty of the hills, Laura thought, *You can't stand here and look at the beauty of the Ozarks without being thankful.*

Feeling her stomach, knowing that life was inside her, Laura closed her eyes. The moment overpowered her. *Thank you, God.* She smiled, then closed her eyes at the world she was bringing new life into.

I want her to be happy, Laura thought. *I want her to have a good life, to love people for what they are, to accept the differences in others.* Then she caught herself.

Her? she chuckled at her assumption. *Why am I so sure it's a her?*

Laura thought of her Pa singing with his fiddle. "Old-time

singing, gladness bringing," and for a moment she felt he was there with her, dancing through the field of grass like they'd done so many times when they were on the prairie.

It's time to tell Manly. A rush of wonderful feelings swept over her and stayed with her all the way back to Mansfield.

Manly came out of Pickle's Barber Shop, rubbing his hands on the short hairs at the back of his neck. He saw Laura parking her car and shouted out, "Hey, honey, wait up!"

"Oh, Manly," said Laura. As he limped toward her, she wondered, *Should I tell him now? What will he say? What can he say?*

"You want to get a bite to eat down at Mom's Cafe?" asked Manly.

"I'm not sure," Laura said, looking away.

"Not sure? You get some bad news from the doctor? You get a flu bug or somethin'?"

Laura shook her head. "No, he said that wasn't it." Laura paused and looked at Manly, then turned away.

Manly frowned. She was acting strangely. "Well, what in tarnation did he say?"

Laura took his hand. "Let's walk for a little while."

Manly limped by her side, feeling uncomfortable holding hands on Main Street. "You sure nothin's wrong?"

"Why do you keep asking?"

"Because," he said, looking at his hand trapped in hers, "we ain't never walked down Main Street like a couple of kids."

Laura dropped his hand and walked ahead. "I just thought you'd want to hold my hand, that's all."

Manly double-stepped to catch up. "Honeybee, hold on,"

he said, limping along. He saw that her eyes were red. "Don't start cryin' on me now. Ain't nothin' the doctor told you that we can't handle together." He grabbed her hand and stopped her. "We've been married for so long that I'd forgotten what holdin' hands meant. Kinda feels good." He smiled.

"Maybe we've forgotten how a lot of things feel," she said, looking away. *How do I tell him that I'm pregnant? He might faint.*

Manly nodded. "Heck, Laura, I'm goin' on fifty years old. I'm an old man. We all forget a few things now and then." He squeezed her hand. "Now tell me what's ailin' you."

"Doc George said something's unusual happening to me at my age."

Manly was suddenly worried. "Things start happenin' to a body when you turn forty, which you almost are. Whatever it is, we can handle it together," he said, very concerned. *Does she need an operation? Is it something serious?*

Laura shook her head. *He hasn't a clue!* She stopped and looked at the children's clothes in Bedal's General Store window. "Doctor said that what I have is just beginning to grow inside me."

Manly's eyes welled up. "You ain't got a tumor, do you?" he cried, putting his arms around her.

"No, I don't have a tumor. That's not what I have."

"Is it something catching?" he asked.

Laura now decided to play with him. "Said I probably caught it in St. Louis."

"I knew it!" Manly exclaimed, kicking the wall. "You probably caught it when you got thrown in jail at the women's votin' rally. I hear you can get all kinds of diseases in jail."

"Nope, that's not how I caught it. He said I probably caught it when we went up to the World's Fair."

"I should have known it!" he frowned. "I should never have let you get near all those people from all over the world. I hear they all carry diseases that can tear the life out of you."

"Nope, I didn't catch it from any of them."

"Well, then, who'd you catch it from in St. Louis?" asked Manly.

Laura put her head against his shoulder. "Doctor said I caught this from you."

"From me!" Manly exclaimed, putting his hands on her shoulders. "I ain't got nothin' catchin' . . . do I?" he asked, now worried that he was sick. "Think maybe I feel hot," he said, feeling his forehead. "Maybe I ought to go see the Doc."

"Doctor said that what's makin' me sick in the morning came from you."

"I don't understand," he said, taking a breath. "Quit playin' games and tell me the bad news. I can handle it."

"All right, I'll tell it to you straight. But first, let me give you a clue."

"What is it?" he asked, impatiently.

Laura looked into the store window. "Do you like those booties?" she asked, looking at the baby clothes on display.

"What do I care about some danged ol' booties? Tell me what disease I got!"

"In a minute," she said, wanting to laugh. "Do you like those baby rattles?"

"Stop talkin' 'bout baby junk, Laura. Unless you're 'bout to tell me that Rose is gettin' married, I ain't got no use for baby stuff."

"I think you do."

Manly stopped and caught his breath. "No."

"Yes."

"No! At our age?"

"Yes," Laura smiled, "at our age."

"Oh, Lord," Manly said, leaning his head against the wall. "I think I'm gonna faint!"

"Come on, Daddy," she laughed, taking his hand. "We got a lot to talk about."

"When . . . when is it due?"

"Not it, the baby. Our baby is due between Christmas and the New Year."

"I'm too old."

"Too late for that," she smiled.

"Where we gonna put it . . . er . . . him?" Manly asked.

"Him?" she laughed. "Are you sure it'll be a him?"

Manly shook his head. "I'm not sure of anythin' anymore. Imagine. A fifty-year old new papa. This'll give the boys at the feed store somethin' new to rib me about."

CHAPTER 18

CHAN'S CHINESE STORE

On her way back to Apple Hill, Laura stopped by Chan's Chinese Store to tell him the good news. He stood up from behind the counter, putting away a book.

"Mr. Chan, I've just come from Dr. George's and . . ."

Chan held up his hand. "Please. I see something." He looked at Laura's face and lightly pinched her cheeks. "Have you been feeling all right?"

"Why . . . yes and no," Laura stammered, caught off guard by the pinch. Chan had never been that open or friendly with her before.

Chan felt her wrist. "Do you know that you're . . ." He stopped and looked into Laura's eyes.

She nodded. Chan smiled. "Are you happy?" he asked, concerned.

"Very happy," she smiled.

"Good," he beamed. "Because I am happy for you . . . and Manly." He felt her wrist again and smiled. Chan walked behind the counter and bent down, then stood up. "You will not think me strange for what I am going to show you?"

"Of course not," she laughed.

"I have something here which will help you."

From under the counter she heard him rummaging around. "Only a few people in town know I sell these. Mostly, I sell by mail to the Chinese scattered in the Ozarks. Ah, here," he said, standing back up, "look at these." He lay down a tray of small jars.

"What's in them?" Laura asked, looking at the strange-looking assortment of medicinal herbs and other things she didn't recognize.

"These are very rare powdered antelope horns, which stop convulsions; and these are pieces of geckos, used for asthma, and—"

"Where did you get these?" Laura asked.

"Very hard to get," Chan said, nodding. "But I get what I need from my cousin Chu in San Francisco, who gets it from cousin Tom Tao in Hong Kong."

"What's this?" Laura asked, holding up an odd-looking twist.

"Those are sea dragon tails," Chan smiled. "Very powerful." Laura made a face.

Chan pulled out another tray which had bits and pieces of things Laura couldn't even guess at. Chan was in a world of his own as he picked through the unusual assortment.

"This is a dried toad, whose powdered skin can relieve heart trouble and these are teas, made from herbs I have found in the hills, and here is a jar of goldenseal mixed with soot and mutton tallow to use on wounds and—"

Laura stopped him. She knew what she saw.

Chan saw her hesitate and smiled. "Yes, these are pieces of snakes. Snakes are very popular with the Chinese. We make medicine from the blood, gall, venom, and skin; we also make soup from the snakes."

"Soup?" she asked.

"Yes, the snakes in Missouri make very good soup." He picked up a jar of snake pieces and started opening it.

"What are you doing?" asked Laura.

"Snake soup is very good for baby." He bowed.

Laura looked at the bits of snake and suddenly felt sick. "Excuse me!" she said, running toward the bathroom.

"I'm so sorry," Chan called after her. When she came back out, looking a little pale, Chan looked concerned. "I was just trying to be helpful."

"I know you were," said Laura, feeling faint. She turned her eyes from the counter. "Would you please put those bottles away?"

Chan quickly put the bottles and trays back under the counter, then looked down and rummaged through another box. He came up smiling, and handed Laura a locket with a gold star on it. "This is for luck," he smiled.

"But Mr. Chan, I can't take this. It's gold."

Chan pushed her hand back. "It is an early new-baby present. I insist that you keep it."

Not wanting to offend him, Laura accepted the locket gratefully and put it around her neck. On her way back to Apple Hill, Laura was hit by a jumble of emotions. Herbs, snakes, and ground-up toads. It all seemed so alien to her. She had never been exposed to any of it.

What is strange to some is common to others. No culture or people are the same, she thought. *But he's a good friend to Manly and me.* She fingered the locket around her neck.

CHAPTER 19

BLINDMAN'S BLUFF

Though he'd tried not to dwell on the Younguns' moving away, Maurice couldn't keep it off his mind. Eulla Mae didn't want him moping around the house, so the only thing she knew to do was send him out to work or walk.

With his work finished, Maurice just decided to walk and think about things to come. On the outskirts of town, he heard the deep moan of a harmonica.

Blindman Thomas, the old sharecropper who'd lost his sight in an accident, sat on his rickety front porch. His grandson, Reever, sat beside him, nodding to the music.

"Hi, Mr. Springer," Reever called out.

Blindman put down his harmonica. "Is that you, Maurice?"

"Sure is," he answered halfheartedly. "Just thought I'd stop by for a minute."

"A minute!" Blindman exclaimed. "If that's all the time you got, then keep on a-goin'."

"Just a figure of speech," Maurice shrugged.

Blindman shook his head. "Too much rush-rush goin' on nowadays. Lot less neighborliness than there used to be. If you don't take time to get out and visit, then you probably don't read the Good Book like you should either. People used to take time to make time. You understand, Maurice?"

"I'm tryin' to follow you, Blindman."

"Good. 'Course these things started dawnin' on me only when my eyes started failin' and nobody came 'round. I used to clutch that Bible every day prayin' for my eyes to keep seein', but when I reached that point where I couldn't read no more, Reever here told me his eyes would see for me, and a peace of mind came over me."

"He's a good boy, Reever is," Maurice said quietly.

"You want somethin' to eat?" Blindman asked.

"No, thank you. I'm not really hungry."

"Well, next time you come by, you got to eat. We may not have fancy food, but for friends, the latchkey is always hung out."

Blindman paused, sensing something was wrong. "What's wrong with you?"

"Just got somethin' on my mind," Maurice said softly, looking away.

"Remember how lucky you are to have eyes that see. Ain't no problem too big to handle if you can see it. Remember that." The old man smiled. His sightless eyes moved without reason, waiting for his ears to locate where to look without seeing.

"This is a problem I can see comin' at me."

"Problems are what you make of 'em," Blindman smiled. "That old talk 'bout an eye for an eye is what's made the whole world blind."

"I'm just in the dumps," Maurice said.

"If you got troubles at home, I got a song for you,"

Blindman said, wailing on the harp. He paused. "And if you got troubles with the taxman or the bossman, I got a song for you," he smiled, running his lips up and down the scales of the harmonica.

"Got any gonna-miss-'em blues songs?" Maurice asked. Reever closed one eye, trying to figure out what was bothering Maurice.

"Sure, I got me a song that will take you away from here," Blindman said.

As the magical music danced out of the harmonica, Maurice let his mind float along. He remembered the good times. *I'm a grown man,* he thought. *If them kids got to go, they got to go.* He nodded. *Uh-huh, yes sir, they were gonna have to grow up sometime anyhow, marry, have kids, move away. Just guess it's all happenin' early so I can get on back to my own life.*

The music stopped. Blindman had the harp perched an inch from his lips. "Don't believe a word you're thinkin'."

"What?" Maurice asked, startled.

"You're just tryin' to convince yourself. Let yourself go. Ain't nothin' wrong with feelin' pain."

Maurice looked into the old man's sightless eyes. For a moment the eyes seemed so clear that he wasn't sure if he they were blind or not. Then they clouded over.

"What are you, a mind reader or somethin'?" asked Maurice.

Reever shrugged. "My granddaddy knows things that can't be explained." He paused. "Some folks say he got second sight. Me, I just think he knows everything about everything." Reever looked at his grandfather with love, awe, and admiration.

"Come here, Reever," Blindman said, reaching out to find his grandson. Once located, he patted the boy on the back of the head.

"Well, you were right on what I was thinkin'," Maurice said.

"Sometimes I am and sometimes I ain't," Blindman said. "It all depends on how the feelin' comes."

Reever whispered to his grandfather. "I got a feelin' that you ain't gonna like what you'll soon be feelin'."

"What's that, boy?" Blindman asked.

"Hey, old man!" shouted Harmonica Preston. "When we gonna settle who's the best harp player in the Ozarks?"

"I best be goin'," Maurice said, sensing trouble.

"No, you sit here. This fool ain't gonna drive my friends away," said Blindman.

"But he looks mad," Reever said.

"Ain't nothin' that a little Blindman's bluff can't handle," the old man chuckled.

Harmonica stormed up to the steps eagerly and took out his harp. "Let's settle this here and now."

Blindman shook his head and put his hand on Reever's arm. "We ain't gonna settle this here and now, here and later, or even in the hereafter. Come on, Reever. Take me inside so Maurice and I can sit a spell. Don't need no big mouth spoilin' this day."

"You can't run forever," Harmonica said.

"I don't run much at all." Blindman laughed. "Don't like to bump into trees."

Reever took his grandfather's arm and walked him into the house. Maurice looked at Harmonica Preston and said,

"Why you two still feudin'? You used to be the best of friends."

Harmonica shoved his harmonica into his back pocket. "I learned how to play from that old man. Yes, I did."

"Then why the fuss?"

"'Cause he told me that the day would come when he'd admit that I was better. Now he won't admit it," Harmonica said, shaking his head.

"Who told you you're better?" asked Maurice.

"Who? It's just somethin' I know."

"Why don't you have a contest or somethin'? Let others decide," Maurice suggested.

"Don't need no contest," Harmonica pouted. "Just listen to us play and you'll know."

From inside the house, the sounds of Blindman wailing on his harp danced through the window. Harmonica took out his instrument and played back an answer.

"You two are crazy," Maurice muttered, walking off.

CHAPTER 20

PICTURES OF THE PAST

Carla Pobst looked at the picture of her late husband, John. Next to it was the telegram she'd received just over two years ago.

Panama Pacific Lines

We regret to inform you that John Pobst was swept overboard during a storm in the Pacific near the Phillippines. All efforts to save him were made, but he was not found. His personal effects will be sent to you.

His personal effects will be sent to you. Carla shook her head. *A telegram says the love of your life is gone, and all you have left is a box of personal effects.*

She opened the box and looked in once again. Everything was still intact. Shaving kit. Shirts. Socks. Writing pad and pen. And a picture. Of John and her standing together, right after they'd gotten married.

When I received the letter, I thought my life had ended. There was nothing left to live for. We wanted to have chil-

dren. I even thought I was pregnant when John left on the one-year trading mission to the Orient. It was only a false alarm.

Carla looked at the picture, holding back a tear. *But it's time to close the past. John, you were a wonderful part of my life, and I'd still be with you today if you were alive. But you're gone. Lost at sea. Dead.*

She closed up the box, after she added the picture of him she'd kept on her dresser since he left on the boat down the Mississippi to the rendezvous in New Orleans with the Panama Pacific Lines. Wrapping the string tightly, then cutting the loose ends from the knot, Carla put the box in the corner with the others to be taken to Mansfield by train.

On her dresser was a picture of Thomas Youngun, whom she had pledged to marry the day after Thanksgiving. With her house in Cape Girardeau up for sale and her personal affairs all in order, Carla felt ready to start her new life with Thomas Youngun in Jacksonville, Florida.

Jacksonville. What will it be like? she wondered. Walking over to the window, she looked out on her back yard. It seemed she was going to another planet. *I've never been out of Missouri, let alone seen the ocean. I wonder if the big ocean will frighten me?*

I wonder if a sea monster will reach out and grab me? she laughed to herself, thinking about the one-hundred-foot octopus they reportedly found on the beach of Jacksonville the month before. *The only octopus I'll be facing is a man in love with me and his three children. That's eight arms I'll have to contend with.*

On the bed was her special suitcase containing the items she would carry on the train. Carla held up the wedding dress that she would wear when she and Thomas said their marriage vows.

In Mansfield, Missouri, Thomas Youngun began a letter to Carla which the trainmaster promised would get to her before she left.

Dearest Carla,

I just wanted to tell you that every morning, when I wake up, you are on my mind. I go to sleep hugging the pillow as if it were you, dream of you in my sleep, and awaken as if every day was the start of the first day of our life.

And again, this morning, you were on my mind. I love you with all my heart and soul.

Yours forever,
Thomas

He looked at the pictures of his late wife, Norma, which were on the bed. *The children have a right to have pictures of their mother, but it's not right for me to keep them on my dresser any longer.*

Putting them away, he picked up the picture of Carla and kissed it. *You are on my mind . . . always.* He smiled and kissed the picture again.

CHAPTER 21

DOG WASHERS

It had been a bad day so far for the Younguns. Larry and Terry were both upset that their father was planning to move.

"You think Pa needs money?" Terry asked his brother.

Larry scratched his chin. "Maybe that's it. He needs money and didn't want to tell us. So he's got to sell the house."

"How much money you think he needs?"

"I guess about what a house costs," Larry said as he shrugged his shoulders.

Terry thought for a moment. "How much does a house cost? 'Bout fifty bucks?"

"At least that," said Larry. "Maybe even sixty or seventy."

"That's a lot of money," Terry said, shaking his head.

"Bet if we gave him sixty bucks, he wouldn't sell the house. What do you think?"

"Might as well be sixty *million* bucks. I only got one cent in my candy-money bank," Terry said.

"Where'd the rest of your money go?" Larry asked.

"I ate it."

"You ate the money?" asked Larry.

"Naw. I gave the money to Mr. Bedal, who gave me the candy I ate up."

"You should learn to share," Larry said.

"You just worry 'bout comin' up with a way to earn some more money."

"Maybe we could *earn* it," Larry beamed.

"You talkin' 'bout doin' some work?" Terry asked. The thought of doing any extra chores totally ruined his mood. *Work? You don't have sense enough to pound sand in a rat hole.*

Rev. Youngun came out onto the back porch and interrupted their pondering. "You boys want somethin' to do?"

"Depends," Terry said.

"I'll give you both a nickel if you wash Dangit. That dog smells to high heaven," said Rev. Youngun.

"That's 'cause he rolled in the manure pile behind the barn," Terry said.

"And ate a dead fish," added Larry.

"You boys want to earn the nickel, or should I just get rid of Dangit?"

"We'll do it, Pa," said Larry.

When their father was back in the house, Terry shook his head. "You can have my nickel if you do the washin'. Last time we tried washin' that dog, we ended up all wet."

"You got to help me," Larry said. "And besides, maybe we can go around washin' people's dogs and earn enough money to buy the house."

"That's a notsaposta."

"What's a notsaposta?" asked Larry.

" 'Work' is a word you're notsaposta say 'round me." Terry laughed smugly. "How many nickels are there in a dollar?"

"Twenty."

"And how many nickels in sixty bucks?"

Larry figured on his fingers. " 'Bout twelve hundred . . . I think."

"Okay, smarty britches," Terry said. "You think there're twelve hundred dogs in Mansfield?"

"Well, there's at least twelve that I know of."

"Twelve's a long way from twelve hundred," Terry said. "Come on. Let's get wet."

No matter how they pleaded, Dangit wouldn't cooperate. "When he gets 'round water," Larry said, trying to corner Dangit, "he's as nervous as a porcupine in a balloon factory."

Finally, they both nabbed the dog and heaved him into the big washtub. But after a minute, the dog jumped out, shook like a wiggleworm and soaked them both.

"Grab him!" Larry shouted, holding his hands in front of his face to block the water. But Terry wasn't quick enough. Dangit ran behind the barn and rolled in the pig pen.

"Now he's really dirty," Sherry commented. She had heard the noise and wanted to watch.

"He stinks worse than a pig!" Terry exclaimed.

"Dangit, you're a dumb dog," said Sherry as she shook her head.

"We'd be better off goin' into the dog trainin' business. This washin' dogs is for the birds," Terry said.

Dangit looked at Larry and cocked his head. "I said *sit,*" Larry commanded.

Dangit just stood there and looked at Larry as if he were crazy.

"Come on, dog, *sit!*"

Dangit wagged his tail and licked Larry's hand. Terry kicked the side of the barn. "He's just a worthless dog."

Larry pleaded. "Please, Dangit, sit 'til we catch you."

Dangit began to wiggle, then rolled over in the mud with his paws sticking up in the air. Terry looked at Larry and shrugged his shoulders. "Maybe he hears things backward or somethin'."

"What do you mean?" Larry asked.

"Well, maybe if you say *sit,* he lays down and rolls over. And if you say *lay down and roll over,* he'll sit." Terry smiled as if he had come up with the most brilliant thing in the world.

Larry shook his head. "That's crazy."

"Try it," Sherry piped up.

Larry thought about it for a moment, then spat at a horse-fly on the fence post. "Listen up, Dangit," he said. The dog laid on his back and wagged his tail. "Lay down and roll over."

Dangit jumped up and began to bark. Sherry laughed. "Maybe he don't understand American."

"What?" Terry asked.

Larry grinned. "She means maybe he don't understand English." Dangit jumped up and licked his face. "Get down you fool dog," he shouted, pushing Dangit away.

Terry kicked the side of the barn again, but this time a bit too hard. "Dangit!" he screamed, jumping up and down on one foot, "I think I busted my toe!"

Dangit, who got upset when someone misused his name, tore after Terry like a bolt of lightning. He grabbed him by the pants cuff and spun Terry around like a top.

"Let go, boy. Let go!" Terry screamed, trying to shake free from Dangit's snarling grasp.

But Dangit was not one to give in easily. It took both Larry and Sherry to pull him free. Finally, after the tug-of-war ended, Terry sat on the ground looking Dangit in the face. "I think this dog's crazy."

"Yeah," Sherry said, spitting into her hands and slapping them together. "I think maybe he has bees."

Terry looked at her as if she were a lunatic. Larry laughed. "She means rabies."

"Yeah!" smiled Sherry.

Terry looked at Larry. "How come you got to explain what she says all the time?"

"'Cause I'm her brother."

"Well, I'm her brother, too, but I can hardly tell what she's sayin' sometimes."

Sherry gave him the once-over evil eye. "That's cause you're 'dopted."

"What?" Terry asked.

Larry shrugged, not wanting any part of what was to come. "She means adopted."

"Yeah, someone left you at the church," Sherry teased.

"Did not!"

Sherry just smirked, knowing she had Terry's goat. "Pa doesn't want to tell you, but you're 'dopted. That's the truth."

Terry's mouth dropped. "I am not."

"Are too," Sherry snapped back. "You're the only one in the family with red hair and freckles. That means you're 'dopted."

Terry was fuming and looked at his sister. "Did you know you're 'bout to adopt somethin'?"

"Oh yeah? Like what?"

"My fist!" Terry shouted, jumping toward her swinging his fist like a wrecking ball.

Sherry took off on a run, screaming, as Terry followed close behind. They went around and through the barn, over the horse pen fence, and slid by the privy before he cornered her on the front porch.

"You're history," Terry said, cocking his fist.

"Pa, help! Help!" Sherry screamed.

Rev. Youngun was sitting in his easy chair going over the church picnic plans. He shook his head and stomped onto the porch. "Terry, stop it! You can't hit girls," he said as he separated the two children.

Terry's fist stopped in mid-air, just seconds from evening the score with his sister. "She was mean to me, Pa. Real mean."

"Was not . . . was not!" Sherry said loudly.

"Hold on, hold on," Rev. Youngun said. "What's this all about?"

"She said I was adopted, Pa."

Rev. Youngun looked at Sherry. "Did you say that?"

"I heard one of the kids at school say that."

Terry began crying. "I'm not adopted, am I, Pa?"

Rev. Youngun picked up his auburn-haired son and wiped his tears. "Of course you're not adopted."

"Then where'd I get my red hair and freckles?" Terry whimpered.

Rev. Youngun smiled. "You got them from my mother's

mother. Your great grandmother had the most beautiful auburn hair you've ever seen."

"She did?" Terry said, wiping back his last tear.

"Yes, she did," Rev. Youngun said, setting Terry back down on the ground. "Now you children go and play. I've got to run back to the church to pick up some papers I left there."

"Pa?" Terry whispered.

"Yes, son."

"Are you really gonna get married?"

Rev. Youngun reached down and picked up his son. "Yes, I am. And we're all goin' to live in a big, happy house together."

"Can't we stay here, Pa?"

"As long as we're happy, it doesn't matter where we live, does it?"

"Yes, it does!" Terry shouted, running away and rubbing his eyes.

CHAPTER 22

LAND SHARKS?

The Younguns sat behind the barn, scheming up ways to keep from moving. No matter how hard they tried, nothing seemed feasible.

Sherry said, "Maybe we should just give up. Pa says we'll like Florida."

Terry cuffed her on the head. "They got land sharks down there! You wanna be eatin' by a land shark?"

"I never heard of no land shark," Larry said.

Terry raised up his hand. "I swear. I was listenin' to some men at the General Store talk about the land sharks in Florida and how they're eatin' everyone up who comes to buy land."

Sherry crossed her eyes and blew air through her lips. "We ain't buyin' no land, so we're safe."

"Oh yeah?" Terry exclaimed. "Then I guess you ain't never heard of alley-gators."

"Have too!" Sherry screamed.

"You listen here," Terry said, lowering his voice to a conspiratorial tone. "We can walk behind the stores in Mansfield and all we got to watch out for are rats and horse droppin's, right?" They both nodded. "Well, in Florida, I heard they got things called alley-gators, which I imagine are kid eatin' monsters who hang out in alleys."

"What they look like?" Sherry whispered.

"I saw a picture of one in the library, and—"

Larry cut him off. "In the library? What were you doin' in the library?"

"It was rainin' and since I couldn't make it to the candy store, it was better than stoppin' in the town square privy to get outta the rain. Okay?"

Larry shrugged.

"Them things in the picture were biggern dinosaurs, at least fifty feet long, and had teeth the size of Bowie knives. And with a name like alley-gator, where else you think they hang out?"

"Why would Pa wanna move to a place like that?" Sherry asked.

"He's been bitten by the love bug," said Larry.

"Hope that bug never bites me," Terry said.

"What else they got in Florida?" asked Sherry.

Terry thought for a moment. "I heard that you can't even walk on the beach without steppin' on sea-needles."

"You mean sea-nettles," Larry corrected.

Terry never liked to admit a mistake. He just kept going. "You're talkin' 'bout another dangerous thing, but I'll get to that."

"What are sea-needles?" Sherry asked.

"I think they're like squishy pin cushions, filled with needles, which are all over the beach at low tide."

Terry had them going and the fact that he believed almost

everything he was saying made him all the more convincing. "And have you heard 'bout Porch-u-geese man-of-warriors?"

"What are they?" Larry asked. Sherry just gulped, holding onto Larry's arm.

"They didn't have no picture of them, but from what I can deduce, it's a bunch of Porch-u-geese men who call themselves warriors. They float around Florida, waitin' for the waves to bring them in. Then they attack, with their stinger knives and bring war on everyone around." Terry paused. "And I hear they like to kidnap little girls and feed them to the sharks."

Sherry gasped with fear. Terry smiled and whispered, "And I ain't even told you about the man-eatees."

"Man-eatees?" Larry said, his eyebrows raised.

"Yes sir," Terry said, raising his hand again. "I swear this is true. Man-eatees are some kind of big fat creatures that wait in swimmin' holes to eat you. In the picture I saw, the one looked like he'd already eaten 'bout four men."

"Maybe we should run away," Sherry said.

"To where?" asked Larry.

"If we go to Florida, we're gonna die," she whimpered, then broke into tears.

"Now you've gone and scared her half to death," Larry admonished his brother.

"Well, thanks a lot!" exclaimed Terry. "This is what I get for tellin' the truth."

"What we need is money to buy the house," Larry sat, putting his chin on his hands.

"Yeah," Sherry said, "and lots of it."

Maurice saw the three of them sitting there and walked quietly up behind them. He'd stayed away for a week, trying to get his emotions in check, but he had promised to give them a ride in his wagon on the first day of school.

"What you kids lookin' so glum for?" Maurice asked. "You upset over school startin'?"

"Naw," Larry said. "We're workin' on ideas."

"Ideas?" asked Maurice. "What kind of ideas?"

"Just ways to earn some money," Sherry said.

"For what?" Maurice asked, suspiciously. "You lookin' for candy money or somethin'?"

Larry shook his head. "If we could come up with some ways to earn money, we thought maybe we could buy the house."

"Buy the house!" Maurice said, wanting to both cry and laugh at the same time.

"That way we wouldn't have to leave," added Terry.

Maurice didn't want to tell them that their plan was hopeless, so he just went along with them. "What kind of ideas you kids come up with?"

Larry shrugged. "We thought about paintin' houses, but we don't have no paint."

"And we thought 'bout sellin' things, but we don't have nothin' to sell," Sherry shrugged, crossing her arms.

"And we thought 'bout raisin' canaries to sell," Terry said.

"Canaries? What do you know 'bout canaries?"

Terry shook his head. "Just know that we decided it'd be better to raise ostriches."

"Ostriches!" Maurice exclaimed. "Why them big birds?"

" 'Cause Larry read me where they eat their own droppin's. Figured they wouldn't cost as much to feed."

Larry frowned. "I told him that idea was worth about as much as puttin' a milk bucket under a bull."

"You all could come work for me after school each day," Maurice said.

Now it was Terry's turn to be suspicious. "You're talkin' *work*-work I bet."

"Sure I'm talkin' *work*-work. Cleanin' out the barn. Fixin' fences. Good, honest work," he said, focusing on Terry.

"That's too hard," Terry said, thinking, *You can count me out.*

"All work's hard," Maurice said, shaking his head. "Terry, sometimes I think you're so lazy that if the hogs were eatin' you up, you'd be too lazy to say sooey."

"Not lazy, just smart." Terry thought for a moment. "There's got to be an easier way to earn enough money to buy the house."

Maurice thought they were dreaming, but decided to go along with their game. "So you want to earn money, right?"

"Yeah," said Terry. "We need somethin' easy to sell. Somethin' that don't take a lot of effort and that we already got."

"You ever thought about sellin' trouble and mischief?" Maurice kidded him.

Larry laughed, warming up to his brother. "He can sell anythin' to anybody. He could sell ice to Eskimos."

"Yeah . . . 'cause he's a good fibber," Sherry smiled, patting Terry's arm. He shook off her hand.

"Good salesmen make a lot of money," said Maurice. "I read in the newspaper 'bout a man in Springfield who's gotten rich sellin' insurance."

"What's insurance?" Terry asked.

Maurice took the wagon around a bend in the road. "That's where someone pays you money so when they die, you'll pay the money plus more back to their relatives."

"What good does money do you if you're dead?" Larry asked.

"Well, it helps pay your burial expenses and all."

"How's a dead man know if he gets a paid-for burial or not?" Larry questioned.

"It's just the way it's done, that's all."

"And that's what insurance is?" Terry asked.

Maurice scratched his chin and said, "You can buy insurance in case somethin' bad happens, like your house burnin' down."

"That's like bettin' on the devil," Larry said.

"No, it's not," Maurice said. "It's just buyin' some peace of mind so in case somethin' happens, you won't lose your mind."

A light went off in Terry's head. "You mean, people will pay you money and then if nothin' bad happens, they don't get nothin' for their money?"

"That's right," Maurice nodded.

"Man-oh-man, that sounds like a great business," Terry smirked, rubbing his hand together. "I want to sell insurance when I grow up."

Maurice tosseled his hair. "Just be a boy for now." He wished the moment could last forever. He wished that they weren't moving away. After he dropped them off, Maurice rode on in silence.

Larry went to play catch with Abe Stern, the Rabbi's son and Terry went over behind the tree, talking to his friend Sweettooth, the baker's son. It was the first recess of the first day of school, and Terry was hard at work starting his new insurance business so he could buy the house.

"Come on, Sweet. I want you to buy some insurance from me."

"For what again?" Sweet asked, eyeing his squirrely friend.

"To make sure nothin' bad happens," Terry said, giving Sweet his most sincere look.

"Bad? Like how bad?"

"You know, like someone stealin' your lunch treat or swipin' the candy from your secret book sack pocket."

"You know about that?" the overweight boy asked loudly.

"Keep your voice down," Terry said quietly.

"How'd you know about my secret candy pocket?"

"I looked. Who you think's been borrowin' your gum drops?"

"Borrowin'? I call that stealin'! I'm tellin' the teacher," he said, standing up.

"And what are you goin' to tell? That you've been sneakin' candy into class when you ain't supposed to?"

"I'm gonna tell that you've been stealin' my stuff."

"Sit down," Terry said, pulling Sweet by the hand. "I ain't been stealin' it, just borrowin' it, that's all."

"You borrowed it into your tummy," Sweet said, disgruntled.

"That's the only place I could think to keep it. I didn't have any insurance, so I didn't want anyone swipin' the gumdrops I borrowed from you."

Sweet scratched his head. "How much would this insurance cost?"

"Well, it all depends on what you got . . . er what you need," Terry said, hoping Sweet didn't pick up on his slip.

"I need to make sure that you don't borrow any more of my candy."

"Well, you're covered there," Terry said, nodding his head.

"I am?"

"Sure. At least for today, anyway. See, your insurance policy is already paid for."

"It is? Who paid it?"

"You, you big dummy. I'm lettin' you let me pay off the candy I borrowed by givin' you one day's candy insurance."

"Gosh," Sweet said, still trying to figure it all out, "that's really nice of you, Terry."

"That's what friends are for," he smiled, patting Sweet on the back.

"Who else you goin' to sell insurance to?" he asked, brushing the dirt from his pants.

"I'm thinkin' 'bout sellin' pigtail pullin' insurance to Brook."

"But you're the one who pulls her pigtails!" Sweet exclaimed.

"And that's why she needs the insurance," Terry laughed, rubbing his hands together. *Man-oh-man, this is going to be a humdinger business,* he thought. *After I buy Pa the house, think I'll buy me a candy makin' machine.*

"Oh-oh, there's the bell," Sweet said.

Inside the schoolhouse their teacher, Miss O'Conner, asked the class, "Did you memorize the months of the year as I asked?"

"Did you?" Sweet whispered to Terry.

"Sure," Terry said, confidently. "January, February, Marchurary . . ."

"Marchurary?" Sweet laughed quietly. "I think you need some brain insurance."

Might have to cancel his candy insurance for that remark, Terry sulked.

CHAPTER 23

NICKEL'S WORTH

Terry thought he'd found a made-in-heaven way to earn enough to buy the house. After school, the kids crowded around to hear his pitch.

"You mean," Little James asked, "that if I give you a nickel, that I'll get good grades on my next report?"

"That's what insurance is for," Terry said, locking his thumbs in the corners of his shirt like he'd seen the tent preachers do. "Now, do you want good grades or do you want to keep your nickel?"

"Do I still got to do homework?" Little James asked.

"That's up to you. 'Course, if I was you and I had good grade insurance, I'd be spendin' my time fishin'," Terry said, tossing an imaginary fishing line.

That was enough to convince Little James, who plunked down his nickel. "Nickel's worth of good grades, please."

Terry reached for the nickel, but Little James closed his hand. "Will this cover *all* my grades?"

"It'll get you a nickel's worth," Terry said, taking the boy's hand and trying to pry it open.

"And how many good grades is that?" Little James asked, struggling to keep his hand closed.

"More good grades than you ever got in your life before . . . now give me the nickel 'fore I change my mind and buy you some flunkin' insurance."

"Flunkin' insurance?" Little James asked, wide-eyed with fear.

"That's right. I control the insurance business in this school, and if I decide to take out some flunkin' insurance on you, you bet your britches that you'll be sittin' with a dunce cap on your head."

"No way!" Little James exclaimed. "You wouldn't do that! We're friends."

"Friendship and business are two different things. Now, do you want the good grade insurance or not?" Terry asked, holding out his hand. Little James plunked his nickel down and scampered off. "Who else wants good grade insurance?" Terry called out. "Plenty of B's still left."

Frenchie Bedal came running up. "All I got is a penny. Can I get a good grade for that?"

Terry rubbed his chin with his right thumb and forefinger. "Can't get an A for a penny . . . but maybe I could give you a B. How's that?"

"Can I have the B in math?" Frenchie asked.

"Done!" Terry smiled. "Now give me the penny before I remember what you did to me at the swimmin' hole last month."

"Sorry 'bout that," Frenchie said, handing him the penny. "I didn't know you were the good grade insurance man."

Terry put his mouth to Frenchie's ear and whispered,

"Don't go tellin' anyone 'bout the good friend discount I just gave you . . . that'd be bad for business."

"Cross my heart and hope to die," Frenchie said, then ran off.

Li Chan shook his head. "That's not right."

"What?" Terry asked without looking up. He was counting his money and thinking about all the candy he was going to buy.

"Selling that insurance," Li said, shaking his head. "You can't promise good grades."

"That's what insurance is for," Terry grumbled. "Now, why don't you get outta here? You're just a bookworm, and you're not good for business."

"I'm not a bookworm," Li said defiantly.

"You'd choose burrowin' into a book over an apple anytime, Worm, so get outta here 'fore I advise you to buy some spit ball insurance."

"Spit ball insurance?" Li asked, then quickly ducked the one Terry shot at him.

Abe Stern, the Rabbi's son skipped up. "Hey, Terry, did you sell Brook some pigtail pullin' insurance?"

"Sure. But if she don't pay me another penny tomorrow morning, I guess I'll have to give her some double-hard pulls after recess . . . maybe even dip one in the inkwell."

"You wouldn't!" Abe laughed.

"Naw . . . I think I'll just cut one off and hang it from my belt."

"You'd do that?" Abe asked, shivering with excitment.

"You just wait. If she don't buy some insurance, no tellin' what bad things might happen to her."

Missouri Poole, the pretty hill girl who was sweet on his brother Larry, tapped Terry on the shoulder. "Pull my pigtails and I'll dunk you in the horse trough."

Terry smiled. "You already got insurance with me."

"I do?"

"Yeah, I'm scared of you," Terry shrugged, running toward home.

When he got home, Terry counted the nickels he'd saved. He didn't hear his father come up behind him.

"Where'd you get the money?"

"Earned it," Terry said, trying to push all the nickels back in his pocket. His father stopped him.

"Earned it? Doing what?"

"Helpin' kids at school," Terry said, not wanting to look his father in the eye.

"Terry Youngun, you better start explainin' yourself."

Terry's eyes welled up. "Me and Larry and Sherry were puttin' our money together into the house-buyin' fund. So I took a job sellin' insurance and—"

"Hold on, hold on. What house-buyin' fund, and who gave you a job sellin' insurance?"

"The money's for you, Pa. We want to buy the house so we won't have to move. Will thirty-one cents do it, Pa?"

Rev. Youngun was moved. He picked up his son and hugged him. "Thirty-one cents is enough to buy my heart for what you children are trying to do."

"We don't want to move," Terry whispered.

"It's just somethin' we have to do. One day, when you're older, you'll understand." He paused and looked into his son's eyes. "What was that about selling insurance?"

Terry's eyes went wide and he gulped. No matter how many ways he tried to explain his new job, his father would have none of it. The next morning, Terry had to go to school and return all the insurance money he'd taken in.

CHAPTER 24

EXTENDED FAMILY

Chan walked slowly to the train station to send a reply to the telegram he'd received from his cousin. He had worried for several days over the responsibility he felt toward his extended family. He wondered what to do with his relatives in San Francisco who needed help and wanted to visit.

Chan's family was proud and wouldn't ask directly for help. Their desire to visit meant to Chan that they needed to move, that they needed to find another place to live. And the mention that they had lost everything was a subtle way of saying they had no money.

The trainmaster had made arrangements for Chan to buy the tickets for his relatives in Mansfield. The tickets would be waiting at the San Francisco station.

If they don't want to come, they can cash in the tickets and use the money for something, and then I will be relieved of any further responsibility. Maybe they can even use the money to get special help for the retarded boy. For a moment he felt ashamed, realizing that he secretly wished they'd use the money for something else.

We Chinese feel such responsibility to our extended fam-

ily, he thought as he caught his reflection in a store window on Main Street. *I have only seen these people once, when they arrived in San Francisco from China. We were leaving for Missouri and they were staying. They could have been anyone, but the old woman, Grandmother Chan, she remembered me from South Mountain.*

He lowered his head at the memory of one who had known his parents. She had known him in another place and time that seemed almost supernatural in his memory.

But my life here is good. My son's life is good. My wife is treated with respect. If it all changes, will the trouble that I read about come here? Will we be driven from our homes as they are in California? What would the people of Mansfield think about a retarded Chinese boy?

"Hi, Mr. Chan," Laura said, approaching him from behind.

"Hello, Miss Laura. Are you ready to play Mah-Jongg again?"

"I'll be ready for our weekly game," she smiled, humming to herself.

"You should be eating snake soup," he said.

"I've got your necklace on," she smiled, showing him.

"Hey, Laura," Lafayette Bedal shouted out from his store. "Congratulations!"

"Thank you, Lafayette," she blushed.

"Was I supposed to say that?" Chan asked, concerned that he hadn't observed an American custom.

"What? Oh, Mr. Chan," she laughed. "That's what we say in America. What do they say in China?" she asked.

Chan paused. "In China we say 'good fortune.'"

"Well, that's good enough for me."

"You should visit my store again. I have some good-health herb medicine that will help your baby grow."

"I don't know, Mr. Chan," Laura smiled. "I don't think I want to eat any Chinese snakes or toads," she kidded.

"No. But I have other things to keep your stomach calm and—"

"Let me think about it . . . okay?" said Laura. Chan bowed slightly. "See you later," Laura smiled, continuing on her way, singing happily. But Laura didn't know that Chan felt hurt.

"That's how we do it in America," he recalled. *"What do they say in China?" "I don't think I want to eat any Chinese snakes."* Chan shook his head. *Will I ever be accepted here?*

Chan was so deep in thought that he didn't see Gorman coming and bumped into the sergeant head-on. "So sorry, Mr. Gorman," Chan apologized pleasantly.

"Watch where you're goin'!" Gorman snapped.

Chan saw the look in Gorman's eyes and his face tightened. Chan said, "I will watch where I'm going. I hope you will do the same."

"Don't talk back to me!" Gorman flared.

Chan paused for a moment. *You are a hateful man, not worth wasting my anger on. But I understand your loss. The loss of your leg.* Chan continued on his way without saying another word.

Chan walked into the train station, having made a decision. He was now determined that if his relatives decided to come to Mansfield, he would make them feel welcome. He would accept them without reservation, even the retarded one.

Gorman clumped along, used to the uneven sound that

the wooden foot made in a shoe he couldn't feel. He turned to watch Chan.

Why do we tolerate Chan and his family livin' here? We ought to form a committee to drive 'em out before more of their kind shows up. They drove 'em out of all the Montana mines. They cleansed Tacoma and drove the heathens out of Tombstone and Tucson, Arizona.

Gorman stamped his wooden foot. A shiver went up his spine. It was like being back in a war. *I've got to defend the town.*

The sounds of racing feet came from behind. Gorman spun around, thinking he was back in another battle. A group of Mansfield children came racing toward him, all smiles and laughter. Gorman looked at the mixture of races and shook his head.

"Hi, Mr. Gorman," Li Chan called out.

Gorman just shook his head. *Get ready to say good-bye.*

CHAPTER 25

THE DECISION

The room was dark. The front windows of Leu Shu-Jen's house had been boarded over. Gunshots sounded in the distance followed by a troop of soldiers galloping down the street.

With the sporadic looting on the outskirts of Chinatown, Yu-Lan and her family worried for Shih Chan, who had gone to the telegraph office. They were also worried about what they would do for food, since their money was quickly running out.

Surrounded by death, destruction, and hatred, the two families had stayed hidden in Leu's boarded-up home, hoping that reason would soon prevail. Surely the madness would end and order would soon be restored.

Tong played with his bamboo-stick man. Though it was one of Yu-Lan's stick dolls with a white powder face, in his mind it was soldier. He had pulled out the dried grass that was the girl doll's hair, which Yu-Lan had spent so much time on, drying the grass in salt.

"Bang-bang," he said, mimicking the gunshots he'd heard outside the front door.

Grandmother Chan played her harmonica softly in the dark corner. Her lips moved slowly, catching each note of the Chinese Opera that she remembered.

As she played, she remembered the mimes and the acrobats performing at the Peking Opera. She smiled at the carnival atmosphere she recalled, the painted faces and costumes of the stage players, and the tinkling music she was trying to play now on the harmonica.

Leu moved the newspaper closer to the candle to read the article again, then put down the paper. It had been weeks since the fifty Chinese had left for the jobs promised in Vancouver. Leu had wanted to go, but his brother and family had persuaded him to stay. Now he was glad he hadn't left.

"Now we can't even go to Vancouver," Leu said.

Yu-Lan and Grandmother Chan perked their ears up. "Is there news about our neighbors who went north?" the old lady asked.

Leu nodded. "Come look at this," he said, laying the newspaper down on the table. Grandmother stopped playing and came over.

Riots Drive 2,000 Chinese From Homes

Vancouver, B.C.—More than 2,000 Chinese were driven from their homes in Vancouver, British Columbia, last night during an anti-Oriental race riot that began as a demonstration staged by some 10,000 laboring men. The attack was a continuation of recent demonstrations against Oriental laborers all along the West Coast.

Police in Vancouver were unable to quell the race riot for several hours, but they finally regained control and made some arrests. In addition to driving the Chinese from their homes, the labor agitators caused about $5,000 worth of property damage. Laborers and others in British Columbia have repeatedly protested the government's encouragement of immigration of Orientals and other foreigners to that area.

Yu-Lan clung to her grandmother's arm. "I don't want to go there," she shivered.

"That appears not to be an option open to us anymore," Grandmother Chan said. She left the room solemnly.

Grandmother Chan went to the back room and picked up the picture of her husband, who had died in the war in China. She thought again about the hardships she'd endured, bringing her children to America to escape the bloodshed. The struggles were not over yet.

Yu-Lan crept in and sat on the floor next to her grandmother for comfort. Glancing at the photograph, she asked, "Tell me about Grandfather."

"He was a good, strong man. I'll tell you about him as a bedtime story."

Yu-Lan gazed at the picture of her grandfather, and wondered what her life would have been like if she had been born in China.

Shih knocked on the door. "Let me in! I have good news!" Leu unlatched the door and let his cousin in. "Cousin Wang Chan has invited us to come and has left paid-for tickets at the station for all of us!"

"We should return to China," Grandmother Chan announced. "Let us give up the dream of the golden mountain and go back to our home. The gods will make Tong better if we return."

"No," Shih said. "We are not going back. There is nothing there for us."

"But we would be with our own kind," the old woman said.

"Mother's right," said Leu. "I'm tired of living in this land where I'm not wanted."

Shih held up the telegraph message. "We are going to the land of promise. We are going to Missouri!"

"Chasing more golden mountains if you ask me," Grandmother Chan said.

"But this one *will* be gold," Shih said, nodding to his family.

The old woman huffed. "Fool's gold. That's all you fools are seeking."

"We have paid-for tickets to get us there," Shih said.

"And you could sell them and use the money to feed us," the old woman said. "You can't eat train tickets, can you?" she asked, leaving the question hanging as she walked from the candle-lit room.

Leu closed his eyes. "If we sold them, we could have a dinner of fish and mussels, mixed with soy sauce, garlic, scallions, and ginger." He opened his eyes and smiled. "We'd have enough money left over to build two more rooms onto this house."

Shih said, "No. We cannot stay here. We will use the tickets to go to Missouri."

"When do you think we can be there?" Leu sighed.

"We will be in Missouri before the first snow," Shih said.

"It will take that long?" Yu-Lan was surprised.

"We have much to do before we leave."

"Will we be there by Thanksgiving?" she asked.

"Thanksgiving?" Leu sneered. "What do we have to be thankful for?"

"We're alive," Yu-Lan whispered.

From the darkness came the sounds of Grandmother Chan's harmonica and her Chinese song. Each note carefully chosen. Her lips moved slowly along the American-made harmonica. Her mind escaped to China.

Tong listened to the sound of gunfire outside, and pointed his stickman at his father. "Bang-bang," he said, smiling.

Leu closed his eyes. "It *is* time to go."

CHAPTER 26

FLYING KITES

Yu-Lan watched the kite float in the air. Her father had taught her how to put the paper on the bamboo frame, making the rectangular kite with the circular opening in the middle.

She had pasted crow's feet on each corner, as she had seen the boys do. Yu-Lan admired the triangular pieces of white paper on the deep blue kite. She liked the way the colors contrasted against the sky.

The wind tugged at the silk string in her hand, so she released another few feet, smiling as the kite bounced in the air, seeming to say, "Thank you." Though the silk burned her fingers slightly as it unrolled, it was part of the sensation of the moment. It seemed to help her understand the kite and the freedom of its flight.

Tong sat on the ground beside her, watching her fly the kite. He was practicing the Pledge of Allegiance that they'd tried to teach him in school.

"I pl . . . ple . . . pledge A . . . A . . . Alle. . . . All egiance to the . . ." He stopped, puzzled.

"Keep going," Yu-Lan said, "you're doing very well."

Tong frowned. "What c-comes next?"

Yu-Lan tugged at the kite to bring it back in line. " 'To the flag,' are the next words."

Tong licked his lips and started again. "I ple . . . pledge . . . A. . . . Allegiance . . . to the flag . . ." He stopped, waiting for her to help.

" 'Of the United States of America,' " Yu-Lan said, shaking her head. "You said it correctly yesterday."

"I forgot," Tong said, bending his larger-than-normal head down.

Yu-Lan felt sorry to have hurt his feelings. "Come on, you can do it."

"I want . . . I want to say it . . ." he paused, groping for words. "I want to say it all . . . the way . . . through. Just once," he said, nodding his head, agreeing with himself.

"You will. Don't you worry. All good things take time," Yu-Lan said. "That's what Grandmother tells us."

The sound of the trains coming and going to the station at the bottom of the hill seemed a million miles away. Up on the hill, the two children were above the trouble that had delayed their leaving San Francisco for several weeks.

Yu-Lan's father plodded up the hill, deep in thought. *He doesn't want to leave mother's grave,* Yu-Lan thought, *but there is really nothing left for us here. I heard him and Uncle Leu whisper about people wanting to ship us back to China or harm us. That is why we cannot stay.*

"Yu-Lan," Shih Chan said, "it is time to get on the train."

"Can't we stay up here a bit longer?" she asked.

"No." He smiled. "If we don't go down now, we may not get a seat. It is a long way to Missouri and I don't want to have to stand." He heard men shouting and turned. He nervously eyed the band of toughs who were massing outside the train station.

Yu-Lan pulled her kite down, then took Tong's hand. "I ple . . . pledge . . . Alle . . ."

Yu-Lan shook her head. "Not now. Someone might get mad."

Tong turned his head to the side, trying to understand. Yu-Lan jerked him along.

Shih took his daughter's hand and said as they walked, "We must be patient. Things will not change overnight." He watched as a band of men harassed a Chinese man, so he guided the children across the hill to avoid them.

"Yes, one day we will all be part of this dream called America. Where all people can have freedom and justice."

"I hope that day comes soon," Yu-Lan said.

"Soon," Shih said, "things will be better. It will be better in Missouri." Shih stopped to hug his daughter. "Look up into the sky. There is a ray of light shining through this darkness which will lead us to the land of promise."

"I ple . . . ple . . . pledge All . . . Allegiance to the . . ." Tong stammered, until the train's whistle drowned him out.

CHAPTER 27

NEW COUNTRY

The cross-country journey renewed the spirits of the two families. Yu-Lan and Shih Chan sat by the windows, looking for landmarks that the conductor had told them about.

Even Grandmother Chan could feel the happiness in the air. The further they got from California, the warmer the people seemed.

"What country you people from?" asked an old farmer who got on in Nevada.

"They're from America. I'm from China," Grandmother Chan answered.

"What part of China?" the man asked.

"South Mountain," the old woman answered, then mumbled, "for whatever good that will do you."

The old farmer smiled. "I was over there in eight-two. Went with the Methodist church. Yes ma'am, I'm familiar with that beautiful part of the world."

"You are?" Grandmother Chan asked, surprised.

"Wish I had some of that shrimp and rice now," he sighed. He looked at the desert flying past the train window. "Can't even get a fresh fish out here."

"Would you like to try some dried shrimp?" Grandmother asked, reaching into her carry bag. She felt the pistol she had hidden from her sons, then pulled out the shrimp.

"You got some?" the old farmer asked. His eyes brightened at the thought.

Grandmother Chan nodded and handed him the small, burlap bag of dried shrimp. "I did these myself," she smiled.

The farmer put one in his mouth and chewed with relish. "Brings back a lot of memories," he said, handing back the bag.

"Please, take more," she bowed, pleased that he liked them.

"Yes sir, I'll never forget bein' in China for as long as I live. I was there before all the trouble started. When everything was really beautiful and peaceful."

"Do you like to read the *bei?*" she asked, pulling out her wooden tiles and clacking them together.

"Sure, but I really love to play Mah-Jongg."

"You do?" Grandmother Chan said in astonishment.

"But I can't find no one to play it with," he smiled. "I just carry it 'round in my sack here and play both sides."

"You have a set of Mah-Jongg with you?"

"Right in here," he smiled, patting his carry bag.

"Let's play!" she said loudly, then looked around to see if she'd disturbed anyone.

Yu-Lan tapped her father in the seat in front of her. "Grandmother Chan has found a friend."

Shih turned and smiled. "We will all find new friends where we are going. It is a new country."

CHAPTER 28

BABY TALK

Indian summer lasted through October. The Apple Hill Farm harvest had been one of the Wilders' best, which was a good omen. A good harvest meant good things to come, and with Laura pregnant, they thought of nothing else but the new baby who would soon enter their lives.

Manly nodded, thinking about the son he thought he would soon have. *Should we call him Manly Junior? Or just Manly?* He thought for a moment. *People would probably call him Little Manly or maybe just Little Man.* He smiled. *Then they could call me Big Man. Big Man and Little Man . . . that'd be great.*

Laura sat knitting in the rocker. *Should I call her Little Laura? Or Little Laurie? Or just Laurie? I know she'll have brown hair and look just like me.*

"Where are we goin' to put him?" Manly asked Laura.

She looked up from the bootie she was knitting. "We'll just keep her in our room."

"Her?" said Manly. "What makes you think it's a her?"

"Just got that feeling," she smiled, waving the pink bootie in front of him.

"Well, I got the feelin' it's a boy, and he won't want to wear no pink booties, that's for sure."

Manly walked upstairs and called out to Laura, "Come up here a minute."

Laura found him standing at the doorway to her sewing room, which was a large storage closet Manly had converted for her. "I think we can put him in here," Manly said.

Laura shook her head. "I don't think she'll like it. There isn't a window."

"Heck," Manly said, "I can just knock a window out right here. He'll love this little room."

Laura crossed her arms. "I don't think she wants to sleep in a closet."

Manly looked at her grumpy expression and laughed. "Honeybee, we're acting like a couple of kids with this he-she stuff. Heck, I'm gonna love the child no matter what it is."

Laura's defenses dropped and she hugged him. "You're right, Manly. That's the way I feel about the baby."

"Good," Manly smiled, taking her by the hand. "Now, we'll put the window for him right here. And I'll hang up a baseball bat and ball over here," he pointed. "And I'll put a football on the shelf here and—"

Laura started to get upset, then burst out laughing. "Manly, you just don't give up, do you?"

"I learned it from you."

Laura kissed him on the cheek. "And I love you just the way you are." She looked around the small room and started pointing. "We'll hang her little dresses here . . . and put her dollies over there and . . ." She stopped. "I'm craving a banana . . . yes, a banana. That's what I want." She kissed

Manly's cheek. "Be a sweetie and run down to Bedal's and get me a fresh, yellow bananna, would you?"

"But I've already been twice today to get you things! You craved a pickle this morning and some butterscotch candy for lunch."

"Can't help it," she smiled, patting her bulging abdomen. "Got to eat for two. Doctor's orders."

CHAPTER 29

CHINESE ARE COMING!

The small-town gossip lines could make a bad rumor worse. When Chan called Laura to tell her that he'd gotten word that his relatives were on their way by train from San Francisco, it was soon all over town.

Though virtually all the townspeople were first- or second-generation immigrants themselves, for some reason, the Chinese were "different" to them. And the Chinese were coming.

Laura had come to town to deliver an article she'd written for the newspaper and headed up Main Street to do some shopping. In front of the Mansfield Hotel, she sidestepped around a group of merchants who were arguing.

"And can you believe it?" Campbell, the Scottish immigrant said. "There's at least six Chinese comin' on that train."

Bedal, threw up his hands. "Where are these foreigners gonna live? This town's already pretty crowded."

Campbell laughed. "You just wait. I hear that where there's one, there's a thousand followin' behind. Soon the whole town will be nothin' but Chinese restaurants and laundries."

Laura walked past them, then stopped and turned. "You men should be ashamed of yourselves."

They turned with a sheepish look on their faces. "Afternoon, Laura," Bedal said, tipping his hat.

Laura walked back and stood in front of them with her hands on her hips. "Just listen to yourselves. Speaking with your Scottish, French, and German accents about foreigners coming to Mansfield."

"But these people are different from us," Campbell exclaimed.

"And how are they different?" asked Laura.

"Why they're . . ." Campbell hesitated under Laura's intense stare.

"They're what?"

"They're different," Campbell said. "They look different from us."

"Different? Because their skin tone is a different shade, or their eyes are shaped differently? Is that it?"

Campbell started to answer, but Gorman marched up and shouted, "That's right. These heathens are different and shouldn't be allowed off the train." Gorman looked at the group. "And if you men care about this town, you'll stand with me on the line of battle to drive them away."

His wild eyes embarrassed the men, who looked away, then down. "Mr. Gorman," Laura said.

"That's Sergeant Gorman to you, traitor," Gorman snapped.

"Traitor? What's come over you?" she asked.

"I seen you trafficking with the enemy," Gorman said coldly.

"The enemy? What on earth are you talking about?" Laura asked.

"Chan," Gorman said, looking around for support. "Chan's Chinese. They're all dangerous. They're the enemy."

"You need help, Sergeant Gorman," Laura said, then looked at each of the other men. "I feel sorry for you . . . for you all," she said, walking away.

At Chan's store, she entered quietly. Chan was sitting at his counter, looking at a chart of some kind. "Hello, Mr. Chan."

"Ah, hello, Miss Laura. Thank you for coming."

"I just wanted to tell you how happy I am that your relatives are coming."

"That is so nice of you." He smiled, bowing slightly.

Laura walked over to the counter. "What's that you're looking at?"

Chan looked down, then blushed. "This? Oh, this is just a Chinese calendar," he said, putting it away.

"Really? How interesting. May I see it?" she asked.

He explained how it worked, why animals represented years, and the history behind it all. Laura stared at the figures of the rat, dog, pig, monkey, and ram around the edges.

"So what year is it now?" Laura asked. "Is this a tiger year?"

Chan smiled. "To deal with the monkey, you must first understand the ram to understand the year that followed . . . the year we are in."

"And what's that?" she asked.

Behind them, the door burst open. Sergeant Gorman stormed in. "You can't keep away from the enemy, can you?"

"Sergeant Gorman," Laura said, walking up and going face-to-face, "you take your crazy thoughts and leave."

Gorman looked at Chan. "I've been watchin' you."

"I know," Chan said coldly, holding back the urge to strike out.

"You're lyin'," Gorman snapped, then smiled. "I should have remembered how tricky you Chinese are."

"Get out of here," Laura said, taking Gorman by the arm.

"Keep your hands off me, traitor!" Gorman looked at Chan and pointed his finger, cocking it like a gun. "Got you in my sights, Chan. You and I got our time comin'."

Gorman slammed the door behind him. "You should go to the sheriff," Laura said as she shook her head.

Chan sat quietly. Finally he said, "The wind carries many things, good and bad. Gorman is a troubled man, and the threats of troubled men are like the wind, they pass by."

Laura thought about the crazy look in Gorman's eyes and shivered. "I still think you should at least tell the Sheriff."

Chan shrugged. "You asked me what the year was on the Chinese calendar." He paused and put his finger on the whiskered animal with the thin tale.

"What year is it?" she asked, looking down.

Chan lifted his finger. "It is the year of the rat."

"Sounds like Gorman's year," she said.

CHAPTER 30

EVERYONE'S AMERICA

Laura couldn't get the incident at Chan's out of her mind. *Gorman could set this town on fire,* she thought. *I heard the men at the hotel talking. The Chinese are coming, but unless something is done, trouble will also come.*

The first chill of approaching winter was in the November air. As the baby inside her grew bigger, Laura wanted to just concentrate on keeping good thoughts in her mind, as the old farm woman had told her to do. But with the grumbling in town over the Chinese, it was hard.

Though Chan hadn't complained, Laura had gone to Sheriff Peterson to tell him about Gorman. The Sheriff had listened patiently, but his hands were tied. Gorman hadn't done anything against the law. All Peterson could do was to keep an eye on Chan when he made his rounds of the town.

An idea came to Laura. Everyone was acting as if the Chinese were the only foreigners in America, so she began to assemble the notes she had kept from her interviews over the years with her friends and neighbors.

Taking up her pencil, Laura sat at her desk and began an article that she hoped would ease the tension in the town.

How Did Your Family Come to America?

With two Chinese families coming to visit our town, I have often thought how quickly we forget our own roots. Just because the Chinese look different and have come from what many think is a mysterious land in the Orient, doesn't mean that how they got here is any different than how any of us got here.

It is a myth to think that America was ever all-English or all-white. It never was or will be, and that's a fact. We are a country made up of Africans, English, Spanish, French, Scots, Dutch, Portuguese, Russians, Canadian, Mexican, Irish. We have come from every country of the world. For this is everyone's America—including the native Americans who greeted our ships as they landed.

Chinese are coming to Mansfield to see what life in our town is like. To see what new friends and neighbors they might have if they chose to live here. So before we start rewriting our history, let's discuss how many of you came to America from somewhere else.

Laura wrote the story about how Lafayette Bedal came from Canada. How the families of the Hardacres came from Ireland. That Rabbi Stern was from Russia. That the Campbells came from Scotland.

Laura wrote from her heart, to dispel the myths people used to justify excluding others. Her words captured the emotions that some had felt when they saw the Statue of Liberty for the first time. Of young children separated from their mothers at Ellis Island. Of their first step on American soil.

She was proud to sign her name to this article. Summers ran it on the front page the next day.

Inside Bedal's General Store, a group of men gathered. Standing alongside the shelves stocked from top to bottom, divided into compartments to accommodate the different shapes and sizes of the goods, the men read the newspaper. They read the article, smiling at the mention of their names or those of their friends.

"You boys want me to turn up the kerosene lamp back there?" Bedal shouted out.

"We can see fine enough," one of the farmers answered.

The party line phone rang and Bedal, who recognized most of the different rings on the line, smiled. "That's got to be Campbell." He picked up the phone and took an order.

Bedal's son, Frenchie, came out from the storeroom. "Father, do you want me to case these eggs you just got in?"

"Test the cream first, then do the eggs."

Bedal hummed a tune while he weighed out the items for a sharecropper who had just moved to town. He put the flour, coffee, sugar, tobacco, and dried beans into the burlap sack, topping it off with the wedge of cheese that he had cut and wrapped.

A young French trapper named Pierre LaPen came in with a string of cleaned rabbits around his neck. "You want rabbits?" he asked in a thick French accent that had taken on some of the twang of the Ozarks.

"Not today," Bedal smiled. "But if you catch some quail or turkey, I'll take 'em. Thanksgivin's almost here."

The men in the back of the store paid them no attention. They were used to Lafayette Bedal speaking French at the drop of a hat with the growing band of French and French-Canadian immigrants who had moved in the area.

LaPen looked at the candy display. "How much are the gumdrops?"

Bedal knew that the young French trapper needed to sell the rabbits to put food on his family's table. He looked out the window. Sitting in a beat-up old wagon were the trapper's wife and three runny-nosed kids, all wearing worse than hand-me-downs. They looked as if they hadn't eaten or bathed in a week.

"You think you can shoot me a couple of turkeys in the next week?" Bedal asked.

LaPen nodded. "Yes sir! I'll shoot as many as you want."

"Six will do," Bedal said.

"Six it is."

"Then I'll advance you a half-pound of gumdrops, and some flour, eggs, milk, and a half pound of bacon. Think that will do?"

LaPen was dumbfounded and just nodded gratefully.

Bedal looked out the window again, then back at the rabbits. "And I'll buy the rabbits."

"But you said you didn't want them!"

"I don't want them, but your wife and kids like rabbit, don't they?" asked Bedal.

LaPen looked down. "Yes. But these are all I have to sell to raise money."

Bedal opened the cash register. "Here, I will give you a dollar for the rabbits and give them to you to eat. Think that is fair enough?"

The young trapper didn't know what to say, and it was all Bedal could do to keep from getting hugged when he handed over the bag of groceries.

"I can't thank you enough," LaPen stammered.

"Just shoot me the turkeys. I never have enough at Thanksgiving."

"You've got my promise," LaPen said. He marched from the store like a conquering hero.

Bedal watched him proudly climb onto his wagon and show the goods to his family. *I got my reward from their smiles,* Bedal thought to himself.

"You sure are a trustin' sort," one of the farmers in the room remarked.

"Can't read the Good Book and not follow its guidance." Bedal shrugged.

Everett Hines, an old farmer from the north county area, shook his head. "Hey, Lafayette, this is a crock, don't you think?"

"What?" Bedal said, closing up his cash register.

"This article by Laura Wilder. I'd say either this woman's a liar or she knows how to tell the truth several ways."

"Laura's no liar, I'll say that for her," Bedal said.

"Then she's not a good American," Hines said. "I spoke to Gorman, who said we got to defend our town against these Chinese foreigners."

Bedal shook his head. "Gorman's crazy."

"He may be crazy, but he's fought against 'em. Told me that every Chinese in this country is a secret agent of the Emperor of China."

Some of the men gathered around and began to nod. Bedal laughed. "That's crazy talk."

"But them foreigners are comin' here!" Hines exclaimed.

Bedal laughed, shaking his head. "We're all foreigners . . . every one of us in this room. I'm from Canada. Jones is from England," he said, pointing to the man next to the cheese wheel. "Campbell is from Scotland. And you," he said, shaking his finger, "Hines, you're from Germany . . . or ain't you the one who buys all the fresh kraut that I make here?"

Hines blushed. "We're different."

"Laura's right," Bedal said. "This is everyone's America. Everyone who comes here legally, this is their country."

Sergeant Gorman peeked through the bushes behind Chan's store. *The enemy's in there. I seen him go in,* Gorman thought nervously, looking around for others.

For a week, he had been scouting Mansfield on his self-appointed protective patrol. He had followed Chan's every move, memorizing his habits, walks, and routine.

I think he's plannin' somethin', Gorman thought. *I think he's an enemy agent, sent here to lull this town to sleep. Then he's gonna open the gates to a horde of yellow people who'll take the town over.*

Suddenly, Gorman ducked down. Li ran behind his father's store. The boy, oblivious to Gorman's presence, tossed his ball up in the air.

Gonna drive all you Chinese out of Mansfield, he thought. From behind him he heard a horse approaching. He crouched down behind the fallen tree, out of sight of Sheriff Peterson who was making his rounds.

When the Sheriff had ridden up over the ridge, Gorman looked back down the hill, but Li had left. *Not gonna let one of them stay in this town.*

CHAPTER 31

THEY'RE HERE!

Gorman stood on the edge of the crowd at the train station. He wanted to get a good look at the new arrivals, the new *Chinese* arrivals.

Gotta see what the enemy looks like, he fumed. *Gotta see their eyes, what their faces look like.*

Laura and Manly stood with Chan and his son Li. "Why is the train so late?" Chan asked, looking at the bright pocketwatch he pulled out from his traditional black robe.

"Mr. Chan," Manly laughed, "it's only one minute late. If it arrives within the next hour, that'll probably be a record."

"Hey, Chan," one of the farmers called out, "how many are comin'?"

"How many what?" Manly asked, knowing full well what the question was about.

"I'm talkin' 'bout Chinese. How many of them Chinese are comin' here?"

"Six," Chan said.

Six! Gorman sputtered in his mind. *Six more of the enemy. That'll make nine, countin' Chan, his wife, and his son.*

Li-Sung Chan saw Gorman staring at him and tugged as his father's robe. "What is it, my son?"

"That bad man is over there," Li whispered.

Laura saw Gorman and walked right over. "What are you doing here?"

"Just mindin' my own business, which is what you ought to be doin'."

"If you're here to cause any more trouble, then I suggest you leave. I've already told the Sheriff about you and your . . . your problems."

"What problems?" Gorman asked suspiciously.

"I think you have mental problems," Laura said. She didn't bat an eye.

Gorman spit in the dirt. "The only problems I got are with traitors like you and Chinese agents like them," he said, nodding to the Chans.

Laura started to speak, but the train whistle drowned her out. Gorman chuckled. "I'd rather listen to train whistles than your hot air."

"Why don't you leave? We don't want you harassing these people."

"It's a free country," Gorman said, "or at least it will be as long as I'm alive."

Laura stared into his eyes, then turned and walked back to Chan and Manly. Gorman watched her. His mind screamed for revenge. *I won't let 'em take me alive. I remember what happened back in China to the men who were captured. I'll go down fightin'!*

Laura watched Gorman out of the corner of her eye. *He's crazy. That man is a lunatic just waiting to explode.*

Gorman began searching the perimeter of the crowd, like

a man looking for something he dropped. Battle sounds were everywhere in his head. *Where is the flag? He looked around. I'm comin', Colonel, I'm comin'!*

The train whistle sounded again and he came back to the present. The sounds of battle faded in his mind. He was able to again concentrate on the enemy that was arriving.

As the train pulled up, Chan nervously adjusted his robe and shook his queue straight. "Are you ready?" Laura asked quietly.

"I am ready," he answered, looking at the train as it came to a stop.

The conductor stepped off and pulled down the stairs. As the passengers got off, Chan looked into the windows. "What if they're not on it?"

"They're on it," Manly said.

"How can you be sure?" asked Chan.

"Look," said Manly, nodding to the faces pressed against the window in the next car up.

Chan looked into the eyes of his six relatives and felt a sense of calm come over him. *I have done the right thing. These are my people. They are family.*

When Shih Chan came into view, he paused at the steps. His eyes locked on his cousin Wang Chan, and he bowed. Wang Chan bowed in return. Li looked between them and feeling the kick from his father, bowed too.

Laura watched as five scared Asians came into view. *I thought there were six?* she thought. Then she saw Tong at the same moment that Chan did.

What's wrong with him? Then she realized that he was retarded. Chan looked at Tong and closed his eyes. *The deformed one. This will only cause problems. What will people in Mansfield think?* But there was nothing he could do, so he maintained his stoic face and greeted his cousins.

"Welcome to Mansfield," Chan said.

Shih bowed. "Thank you for making it possible for us to come here."

After the family was introduced, Chan turned to Laura and Manly. "I'd like to introduce you to my good friends Laura and Manly Wilder."

Shih, Leu, and their families looked at the white faces. Grandmother Chan stood behind, eyeing the sea of white faces around her. *This will never work.*

Then she saw Gorman and felt the hair raise on her neck. *That is a real devil. He is an evil one.*

While Laura and Manly made the new arrivals feel welcome, they didn't see Gorman start forward. He looked at Shih, then Leu, then Ko, then the old woman. He saw Yu-Lan and then stopped dead in his tracks.

He saw Tong.

"You heathens ain't welcome here!" Gorman shouted, not taking his eyes off Tong.

Shih and Leu put their hands up to protect their family. Wang Chan turned, his eyes burning with rage at the humiliation.

Laura stepped between them. "Leave now, Mr. Gorman. These people are welcome here."

"Who says? You?" he sneered. "You're just a Chinese lover." Gorman looked at the crowd that was gathering around. "Me? I don't want more Chinese here. Specially no heathen Chinese."

Chan stepped in front of Laura. "These people are Chinese Methodist Episcopals. If they're heathens, then so are you."

"Who ever heard of Chinese Methodist Episcopals?" Gorman laughed. "That's just a cover so they can take over the town."

Manly cleared his throat. "Gorman, I feel sorry for you. We all do," he said, looking around the crowd. "But if you don't leave, I'm gonna call the Sheriff."

Gorman limped forward and Manly limped toward him. Gorman said derisively, "Least my limp's from defendin' my country. What's yours from? Steppin' on a chopstick?" Gorman laughed, looking around, but no one joined him.

Manly leaned toward Gorman's face and whispered, "I ain't a fightin' man, but if you don't leave, I'm gonna open everythin' that's closed and close everythin' that's opened on your face."

Gorman pointed to Tong. "What's wrong with the ugly one?"

Tong just smiled. Whenever he sensed trouble or couldn't understand something, he withdrew into himself.

Yu-Lan felt the tears coming and put her arm around Tong. "Leave him alone!"

Tong began to speak softly. "Gi . . . Gi . . . Gift fro . . . fro . . . from—"

"What's he tryin' to say?" Gorman laughed.

"That he's a gift from God," Yu-Lan cried.

Leu felt the pistol under his robe, wondering if he should pull it out. Grandmother Chan saw his fingers nervously outline the trigger and walked over. She whispered, "There is no need. We are safe. He is just a crazy devil."

"Gift from God?" Gorman laughed. "Not *my* God!"

"This has gone far enough, Gorman!" Manly said, taking Gorman by the arm. "It's time for you to leave."

Gorman shook off his grip. "I'm leavin'." He turned and stopped, slowly spinning around on his wooden leg. "But I'll be back," he said to Wang Chan and his relatives, pointing and cocking his finger like a gun. Then he left the platform.

"I'm sorry for what happened," Laura apologized sincerely, as he walked away.

"It is all right, Miss Laura," Wang Chan said. "You cannot be blamed for what he has done."

"He's just a bad apple," Yu-Lan mumbled.

"What child?" asked Laura.

"They taught us in school that one bad apple can spoil the barrel," Yu-Lan said quietly.

Grandmother Chan looked around. *Looks like the whole barrel is already spoiled. The whole golden mountain is spoiled for the Chinese.*

Then she thought of the nice old farmer who'd played Mah-Jongg with her all the way to Kansas. *I cannot judge all white people by this crazy man here,* she nodded, wishing she could find a peaceful place.

CHAPTER 32

MUSIC EYES

The Chan house was very crowded, but no one seemed to mind. Laura and Manly had come for the welcome celebration along with a dozen neighbors who had brought food and small gifts.

Their gestures made up for Gorman's insults and soon Shih, Leu, Ko, and Grandmother Chan were feeling the warmth of Mansfield.

Yu-Lan and Tong sat on the back steps, glad to be away from the talkative adults. "You want to do something?" she asked Tong.

"Yes," Tong smiled. "Wh . . . what?"

Yu-Lan thought for a moment. "Why don't we fly our kite?" she smiled.

"Can I fl . . . fly it?" Tong asked hopefully.

"Why don't you let me get it up in the air first, then you fly it."

Tong clapped his hands twice. Yu-Lan went inside and slipped along the edge of the room, trying not to be noticed by the adults.

"What are you doing?" Grandmother Chan asked as she reached the bedroom doorway.

"Tong and I are going to fly my kite."

"Where?" the old woman asked. "There are too many trees around here."

"Li said there's a field just over the hill. That's where we'll be."

Grandmother Chan thought of Gorman. "I don't think you should go. It's too dangerous."

Yu-Lan giggled. "Grandmother! This is not San Francisco. This is Mansfield. The land of promise."

Grandmother Chan thought, then relented. "Just don't go away too far. Your father will be worried."

Yu-Lan unpacked her kite and crept out to the back. "Come on!" she shouted to Tong. "Let's go." She grabbed his hand and walked as fast as he could safely go.

When they came to the field, Yu-Lan unfurled the kite and put it into the wind. Tong squealed with joy as the kite took to the air, flapping in the strong breeze.

"My . . . my turn," he stammered.

"Here it is." She smiled and held out the string. "Take it."

This was the first time she'd ever let Tong fly the kite without her holding onto the string. There was just something about the day, the beauty around them, and the town they were in that made her do it.

Grandmother Chan slipped out the back door to walk. *Too much talking.* She shook her head. The pistol was hidden under the waistband of her robe.

I don't know why I carry it around, she wondered, shaking her head. *I've never even fired a gun.*

She saw Yu-Lan's kite high above the trees and tried to

figure the way there. She wasn't more than a block away, when she cut through the alley and onto the back road that edged the town.

Every time Grandmother Chan thought she had a clear path to the kite, the wind changed and blew it in a different direction. *I do not want to get lost.*

With each step, she memorized landmarks so she could find her way back. It was a habit she had gotten into since first coming to America, when she couldn't read the signs in English.

Gorman watched her from the woods. He stepped in the shadows, dressed in his old battle uniform. His rifle was loaded and his mind was clear. The sounds of battle had not yet begun to throb and pound his mind.

The sound of a harmonica drifted through the woods. Grandmother Chan smiled, drawn to the music, forgetting about Yu-Lan and her kite for the moment. *That must be a trained musician,* she thought. But as she crested the small hill, she was surprised to see an old black man sitting by himself on the front porch of a rickety home.

When Blindman finished playing, Grandmother Chan clapped loudly. "Who's that?" Blindman called out.

Grandmother Chan didn't know what to say. "Well, if you won't speak, then you can listen. Just know when it's the right time to clap." He laughed and began playing again.

Grandmother Chan hesitantly moved toward the porch. She sat down on the step and listened to the music.

The old woman took out her harmonica and began playing along. Blindman stopped. "Who're you?"

Grandmother answered quietly, "I am an old grandmother." She did not realize he couldn't see her.

Blindman turned his head. "Well, I'm an old grandfather and my grandson is in town buyin' groceries." He paused and played a short riff. "Where'd you learn to play the harp?"

"In California," she said.

"You got a funny accent, but if you can play, then follow this." He began a toe-tapping harmonica flight of fancy. Grandmother Chan followed along, playing as she felt.

After a few minutes, Blindman stopped and smiled. "You're good! How long you been playin', you said?" he asked, looking around to where he thought she was sitting.

"I am over here," she said softly.

"Well, sometimes it's hard for these old blind eyes to see you."

Only then did Grandmother Chan know he was blind. *That is why he didn't object to my presence,* she thought.

"I have to go," she said, putting her harmonica away.

"Where you goin'? We just started playin'." He paused, sensing something was wrong. "It's okay that you're different. Heck, we're all different in our own way."

"But I am Chinese and—"

"And I'm a blind old black man. So what does that win us? Couple of train passes to the white city of your choice?" he laughed.

Grandmother Chan felt a sigh of relief. "I did not want to burden you."

"Burden? It's a pleasure havin' someone to play with besides Harmonica Preston. Just 'cause you're Chinese, don't make you less human than the next person."

Grandmother Chan cocked her head. "But being Chinese is hard here."

"It all depends who's where in this old world." He chuckled. "You know, this 'majority rules' thing is a two-headed dog." Blindman picked up his harmonica. "You ready to play?"

She nodded.

"What? Can't hear you."

"Sorry," she blushed. "Yes, I am ready."

"Then you pick the song."

Grandmother Chan thought for a moment. "Do you like Chinese Opera?"

"I don't know. I ain't never eaten Chinese food, so I certainly don't know what the opera is." He thought for a moment, then smiled. "Matter of fact, I ain't never been to *no* opera in my life."

"It sounds like this," she said, then began playing.

Blindman nodded his head to the music. "Heck, just keep on playin' and I'll fake it," he laughed, letting his mouth fly along the harp a note behind.

He has music eyes, she thought, feeling the glow of happiness overtake her.

There were now two people watching the fun they were having. Gorman was back in the heat of battle, and Harmonica Preston stood on the other side of the house. Preston shook his head.

Gorman carefully aimed his gun sight at Grandmother Chan. But she was moving her head to the music, making it hard for Gorman to keep her in his sights.

Then the bombs went off. He looked around, but saw nothing. *Must be in my mind.* He tried sighting back down again, but he thought a bullet whizzed over his head.

Gorman put down his rifle and wiped his brow. *Got to get control of myself. Can't lose sight of the enemy.*

Gorman aimed again. Harmonica walked into his view. *Who's that?* Gorman wondered, trying to sight around him. *That's the black man from Pickle's Barber Shop, Harmonica Preston. What's he doin' here?*

"Hey, Blindman!" Harmonica shouted out.

Blindman stopped playing. Grandmother Chan suddenly felt embarrassed. *I am a widow, sitting on a man's front porch.* "I must leave now."

Blindman reached out and took her arm. "No need to be packin' up. We were just startin' to get down on that Chinese Opera."

"Blindman, I'm talkin' to you," Harmonica said as he came up the stairs.

"What you want?" Blindman asked indignantly. "Can't you see we're makin' some real good music?"

"Who's she?" Harmonica asked, looking at Grandmother Chan.

"She is a friend of mine. So if you don't mind, I'd appreciate your leavin' us alone." He put the harmonica back to his lips and began playing where he left off.

Harmonica was furious. "Are you gonna accept my challenge to see who's the best harp player in the Ozarks?"

Blindman stopped playing. "Don't listen to this fool," he said to the old woman. "He just wants to have a harp playin' contest and . . ."

Grandmother Chan spoke without thinking. "We accept."

"You do?" Harmonica said, dumbfounded.

"Who's this we stuff?" Blindman asked.

"We should play. Music is better than talking," she said.

"Where and when?" Harmonica asked.

"You pick the time and place. We will be there," Grandmother Chan smiled.

"Lady, I don't know who made you my keeper, but count me out of this," said Blindman.

"You are a wise man," she said back. "You know more than people with eyes know."

"Music I know. Don't need eyes for that," Blindman huffed.

"But you have music eyes," she nodded. "You understand the harmony of life. Like Confucius, you—"

Harmonica shook his head. "Confucius? I'm confused."

"Trust me," Blindman said, "so am I."

"Okay," Harmonica laughed. "We're gonna find out who's the best." He took his harp out. "Now let me play some of this Chinese music."

Gorman moved the rifle back and forth, trying to get a clear shot. *Come on, Harmonica, move it!* He tried every angle, but couldn't get a clear shot.

Guess I'll just have to take the next one I get, he thought, concentrating on the straight shot he was waiting for.

CHAPTER 33

DANGER

"Maurice, you look like you're feeling better," Laura said, as they stood in front of Chan's house.

"I've been talkin' some with Blindman. He's been helpin' me some."

"Everything's going to work out," Laura said.

"You ought to go see him," Maurice nodded. "Give you some insight into what's goin' on between everybody in this town."

"I think I will." She smiled, then said good-bye. She told Manly that she wanted to take a walk.

"Sure you're up to it?" Manly asked.

"I'll just take the backroad toward Blindman's house. Why don't you get the groceries and pick me up on the way back?"

"Just be careful, Honeybee," Manly said, kissing her cheek. "I don't want anythin' to happen to Manly Junior in there," he smiled and patted her tummy.

Laura walked along through the woods, thinking happy thoughts. She saw the beautiful kite flying in the air, and for a moment she was back on the prairie with her father, play-ing the games he'd taught her.

As she neared Blindman's house, she waved to Harmonica and Grandmother Chan, who were walking back toward Chan's. "Is Mr. Thomas at home?"

"Mr. Thomas?" Harmonica laughed. "If you mean Blindman, yeah, he sure is."

Grandmother Chan bowed to Laura. "I want to thank you for the friendship you have given to cousin Wang Chan."

"You mean, Mr. Chan?" Laura smiled.

"Everybody's a mister to you," Harmonica laughed. He turned to Grandmother Chan. "Come on, Grandma, let's make some music."

Grandmother Chan shook her head. "I have to find my granddaughter and grandson now. They went out to fly a kite."

"There's a trail just over the hill that leads up to the field. I'm sure that's where you'll find them," Laura said.

Grandmother Chan, Harmonica Preston, and Laura parted ways. When Laura got close to Blindman's she saw him sit-ting on the front porch by himself. "Who's comin'?" he called out, hearing the crunch of leaves.

"It's Laura Wilder," she answered. "Seems you got to meet one of our new neighbors."

Blindman smiled. "She plays a good harp." Laura watched his fingers grope around the wooden boards around him. "She left these here," he said, holding up the wooden *bei*.

"If she doesn't come back, I'll take them to her tomor-row," Laura said, taking the *bei* from Blindman. "Did you like her?"

"She seemed nice enough. Can't understand what all the fuss is around town 'bout them comin' here."

"These poor people," Laura said. "Their homes destroyed by an earthquake, driven out of California by hatred, and now this."

"Might not be the last of their problems," Blindman said to himself.

"What?"

"I said, this might not be the last of their problems. Feelins in this town against the yellow people are runnin' higher than against us black folks." He paused, shaking his head. "Course, bein' blind makes all this color talk seem sort of foolish."

"What can we do, Mr. Thomas?"

Blindman smiled. "It takes time, but sooner or later people are gonna realize that color is only skin deep. Heck, I've always found that if you let people touch each other, they'll find that they don't bite," he laughed, suddenly reaching out and taking Laura's hand.

Laura relaxed as he touched her fingers lightly.

"Think of it as feedin' pigeons in the park," Blindman said. "You can only get so close, but no closer. You can step toward them and the pigeons step back. You can step backward and the pigeons step forward. You don't never get any closer or farther away. And that is the problem between colors."

"I don't know what we can do about it," Laura said.

Blindman let go of her hand. "I don't rightly know either. So if you and I have trouble talkin', imagine what it must be like for them Chinese who don't hardly know the language."

In the woods above them, Gorman watched. His wild eyes

darted around. I didn't count on Laura Ingalls Wilder being here. *But she's turned out to be one of them.*

Gorman smiled, unslinging the rifle from his soldier. The sounds of battle raged in his fevered mind. "I'm goin' in, Colonel!" he blurted out.

Laura's face snapped up toward the woods. "Gorman? Is that you, Gorman?"

Gorman sighted and shot, but Laura was doubled over by a pain in her stomach and the bullet just grazed her head. She fell onto the wooden porch, moaning.

"You all right?" Blindman shouted, feeling with his hands to find Laura.

Another shot rang out just as he found her, and he lay on top of her to protect her. His hands felt the blood trickling down Laura's scalp. "Oh, Lord," he whispered, "don't let this woman die."

A sickening, helpless feeling came over him. Old and blind. There was nothing he could do to stop what was coming. All he could do was shield Laura, hoping that help would arrive.

"My head," Laura moaned.

"You're alive," he said, pulling his handkerchief out and holding it to where he felt the scalp wound.

Blindman heard the crunch of leaves as Gorman started down the hill. "He's comin'," he said, turning his head toward the sounds, helplessly.

Laura looked, her eyes blurred. But there he was, coming down the hill with the rifle in his hand. "I'm gonna kill the traitor," he shouted.

Laura stood up, holding onto the porch beam. "Gorman, stop this!" she screamed. "This is madness!"

Gorman laughed and kept coming toward her.

"Leave us alone," Laura pleaded, doubling over with a pain in her stomach. *Think happy thoughts for the baby,* she told herself. But there were none in her mind.

Gorman stepped onto the porch, pushing Blindman out of the way. He grabbed for Laura, who tried to duck and avoid him, but fell from the porch.

The pain was so bad that she thought she was dying. *The baby,* she thought, *please don't hurt the baby!*

"Get up!" Gorman screamed, grabbing her arm.

A shot rang out behind him. "Leave her alone!" Grandmother Chan shouted, holding the pistol in front of her.

Gorman turned. Raising his rifle, Gorman backed away. "Don't come no closer."

"Leave or I'll shoot you," Grandmother Chan said with quiet intensity.

Gorman sneered. "I'll be back," then ran away up the ridge.

Grandmother Chan put the pistol back into her robe and ran to help Laura. "My baby," Laura moaned. "Don't want to lose my baby!"

The old woman felt Laura's stomach. "We need to get you to the doctor." Laura moaned and Grandmother Chan saw the locket that Chan had given Laura.

"Mr. Chan gave it to me," Laura said.

"It is a good luck symbol," the old woman nodded. "Everything will be all right."

"Why did you come back?" Laura asked.

"I left something here," Grandmother Chan said, looking around.

"I think these are yours," Laura said, gritting her teeth in pain and squeezing the old woman's hand as she handed her the *bei*.

Manly drove over the hill and pulled into the drive. "Oh, Lord," he moaned when he saw Laura. "Is she hurt?"

"Get her to a doctor," Blindman said. "And get me outta here."

Manly lifted Laura into the car, then helped Blindman and the old woman in. "Hold on, Laura, I'll have you to the doctor's in no time."

Please let my baby be all right, Laura prayed, biting back the pain.

CHAPTER 34

THE PLEDGE

While Manly rushed Laura to the doctor's, Gorman ran through the woods, bumping into trees. His mind was lost between the old battle and where he was now.

I won't let 'em take me, he mumbled, looking for a place to hide. Then he saw the kite. Something about it reminded him of the colorful days in China, when the Chinese children at the mission greeted the arriving soldiers.

A state of confusion came over him. He couldn't decide if the kite represented the enemy or the friendship that he'd been shown by the Chinese children.

Then he thought about the battle again, and knew they were the enemy. Following the kite, Gorman came upon the field where Yu-Lan and Tong were playing.

"Tong, you're doing great!" Yu-Lan clapped. She adjusted her hair ribbons and squeezed his shoulder.

Tong smiled and watched the kite. "It is ver . . . ver . . . very pretty."

Gorman crept along the edge of the clearing. *That must be a signal kite. Must be some message they're sendin' to the rest of 'em hidin' in the hills.*

Yu-Lan lay back in the grass to enjoy the warmth of the sun. "I'm so glad we came here," she said, closing her eyes. "Everything's going to be just fine here."

Tong saw the soldier creeping toward him. He gripped the kite string, not knowing what to do.

"If I fall asleep, you better wake me," Yu-Lan yawned. "And don't let go of the kite, whatever you do."

Tong tried to speak but he couldn't get the words out. Gorman stood up and pointed his rifle at the boy. He put his finger to his lips for quiet. Tong nodded that he understood.

Yu-Lan felt something press against her face and opened her eyes. She was looking straight into the barrel of the rifle.

"You're comin' with me," Gorman said, grabbing her arm and pulling her up.

Tong stepped forward. "No! No! No!"

"Shut your mouth," Gorman snapped, setting his rifle down.

"Leave me alone!" Yu-Lan shouted, then began screaming. In her struggle, her hair ribbons came loose.

Gorman put his hand over her mouth and carried her off toward the hill to the north. He tripped on a rock and fell down, knocking Yu-Lan unconscious.

Tears crept down Tong's cheeks. He looked at Gorman's rifle. *Must follow . . . must follow Yu-Lan,* he thought, and took off as fast as he could go, holding onto the kite.

After taking Laura to the doctor's, Manly went straight to see the Sheriff. They went to Wang Chan's house to get their help.

Chan and his cousins sat in his living room, sharing stories and experiences. "I hope Grandmother doesn't get lost," Leu said.

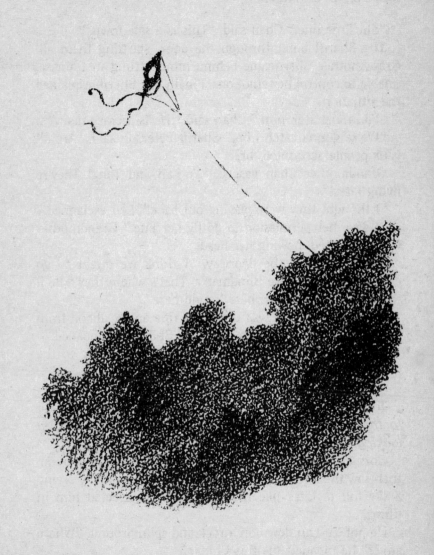

"She'll be fine," Chan said. "This is a safe town."

The Sheriff burst through the door, startling them all. Grandmother Chan came behind him, rattling in Chinese, unable to control her emotions. Finally the Sheriff explained the situation.

"You must stop him," Chan said. "He is a crazy man."

"We're gonna catch him," Sheriff Peterson said. "Are all your people accounted for?"

Grandmother Chan gasped. "Yu-Lan and Tong! They're flying kites!"

"I thought they were playing out back!" Leu exclaimed.

"I gave her permission to go fly her kite," Grandmother Chan admitted, bowing her head.

Manly stood in the doorway. "I think we ought to go check that field above Blindman's. That's where they'd be if they're flyin' kites anywhere 'round here."

But all they found was Gorman's rifle and a ribbon from Yu-Lan's hair. "Where can they be?" Shih Chan moaned.

"They're up there," Grandmother Chan pointing to the kite flying above the trail in the woods.

Tong followed behind Gorman as best he could. *Hold on to the kite,* he kept telling himself. *Don't stumble. Keep looking.*

Gorman stopped halfway up the hill and looked around, then saw the kite. *It's followin' me!* he said, suddenly seeing a sky full of kites like the ones that had greeted him in China.

He put Yu-Lan down on a rock and spun around. "Where am I?" he moaned. "Is this China?"

The edge that he had been wavering on for so long had been crossed. Gorman had lost all touch with reality.

Tong came up quietly and walked over to the unconscious Yu-Lan. "Wake up . . . wake up," he said, rubbing her cheek.

Yu-Lan opened her eyes. "Tong . . . that man . . . where . . ." then she saw Gorman. He was on the edge of the cliff, looking down.

"Let's go," Yu-Lan said.

Tong handed her the kite, then ran to where Gorman was standing. "Don . . . don . . . don't jump," the boy said.

"What? Who are you?" Gorman shouted, acting as if he were surrounded by many people.

"I am Tong . . . pl . . . pl . . . please don't jump. Gi . . . Gi . . . Gift from God."

From behind them, the Sheriff crept up and grabbed Yu-Lan, shoving her behind him and silently covering her mouth. Her father hugged her, but kept the silence the Sheriff had insisted upon.

"Gorman," Sheriff Peterson shouted out. "Gorman, get down from there."

"Tong, come here," Leu whispered to his son.

Tong stepped up onto the edge with Gorman. "Come . . . come down."

Gorman looked at him, cocking his head back and forth. The Sheriff moved in closer. "Come on, Gorman, the war's over. You just need a little rest. That's all."

"He's a kite boy," Gorman smiled, looking at Tong.

"Yes, he is," the Sheriff said, not understanding what Gorman was talking about.

"Don't think I should be taken alive," Gorman smiled.

"Why?" the Sheriff asked, moving up within six feet of the two on the edge.

" 'Cause that's what the Colonel said," Gorman nodded.

"You're a good soldier, Gorman," the Sheriff said, lifting Tong from the edge and setting him down farther back.

"I'm a good soldier," Gorman said, saluting toward the Ozarks in front of him.

"Don't jump," Peterson said.

"Good soldier," Gorman mumbled.

Don . . . don . . . don't jump, good soldier, Tong thought. Getting his courage up, he shouted as loud as he could. "I ple . . . ple . . . pledge Allegiance to . . . to . . . to the flag . . ."

Gorman turned, saluted Tong, and began reciting the pledge with him. Sheriff Peterson mumbled along with them as he inched toward Gorman.

As if handling eggshells, Sheriff Peterson took Gorman's hand and helped him away from the cliff. When they got to Tong, Gorman saluted him again.

"At ease, soldier," Gorman said.

Tong nodded and took Gorman's other hand.

"What will happen to him?" Wang Chan asked Manly.

"There's a hospital up in Springfield for sick folks like Gorman. That's where he'll be sent, most likely."

CHAPTER 35

BUYER BEWARE

Dr. George took a sip of water. "You took a bad fall, Laura," he said, shaking his head.

"Is the baby all right?" she asked weakly from the narrow bed in his office.

"Hope so. Never know when you take these kind of falls. Baby's due in less than a month. It could come any time now."

Laura tried to think happy thoughts. "I hope they find Gorman before he hurts someone."

"Don't you be thinkin' 'bout him. Just rest your mind for a while." He sat down on the straight-backed chair next to the bed and checked her head bandage again.

Manly came in and told them about Gorman's capture, then asked, "What should I do? Can I take her home?"

"Think you ought to take her over to the hotel and let her rest. I don't want her travelin' far in her condition."

"Think I ought to let her just stay in town until Thanksgivin' dinner tomorrow?"

"I don't know if she'll feel much up to eatin'," Dr. George said.

"If I'm not cooking, I'll be hungry," Laura said weakly with a smile on her face.

With Laura's health under control and Tong and Yu-Lan safely home, there was plenty for Manly and the Chans to celebrate. But Rev. Youngun was the happiest man in Mansfield. Carla Pobst had arrived on the noon train from Cape Girardeau, and they had gone for a buggy ride.

"Oh, Thomas," Carla said, hugging and kissing him the moment they were out of sight.

"Carla, hold it a minute," he laughed.

"Just drop the reins, you silly goose," she said, nuzzling against his ear.

Unable to hold back, Rev. Youngun dropped the reins and hugged and kissed Carla, while the horse just continued on his way home. It was just like his dreams.

Back at the house, the Youngun children hid themselves behind the barn, watching the buyer who had come back for a third look at their house. "This man's serious," Larry moaned.

"Pa said he thinks this is the one," added Terry.

"Feel like kickin' him in the leg," whispered Sherry.

The man had brought his whole family along, which made it worse. "Look at them kids," Larry said.

"I bet they touched my toys," said Terry.

"Got me an idea," Larry said. "Come on in the barn."

"What you got in mind?" Terry asked.

"Look. Remember that time last year when we made that mountain screamer from a nail keg and hide?"

Sherry nodded. "'Bout scared me half to death. I thought it was a monster."

"That's right. It sounds like a bull and a mountain lion fightin'."

"You still got it?" Terry whispered.

"I hid it in the hayloft. I wanted to scare you all at Halloween with it."

"Let's try it out," said Terry.

Larry climbed up and got it out. The hide was still taught on the nail keg. The thick string was still hooked to the button in the center of the hide, which made a terrible noise when you pulled hard on it.

Larry took the mountain screamer out behind the barn. He held it up and whispered to Terry, "Pull hard on the string."

Terry gave it a small tug and the sound that came out was frightening. "Pull harder," Larry said.

Terry pulled with all his might and it sounded like a mad bull fighting with a mountain lion. The man and his wife went ashen-faced on the porch stairs. Their children ran screaming from the yard and all the animals in the barn began screeching.

"What was that?" asked the man's wife.

"Sounded like a monster," said his son.

"Pull it again," Larry whispered.

Terry pulled it with all his might and the mountain screamer roared again. Crab Apple the mule kicked down his stall door and bolted from the barn, followed by Lightnin' the horse, Bessie the pig, and T.R. the turkey. They could hear Beezer the parrot squawking for dear life inside the house.

With all the noise from the animals and one more pull on the screamer, the family on the stairs were huddled together.

"Where's Bashful?" Terry asked, peeking into the barn, trying to see where their fainting goat was.

"He's down for the count," Larry said. He pointed to the goat, lying on its side.

"Pull it one more time. Then, Sherry, I want you to go up and talk to them," said Larry.

"'Bout what?" asked Sherry.

"See how they like the thought of movin' into a haunted house with monsters around."

When Terry pulled it again, Dangit the dog came running into the yard, howling as if he were being chased by the devil. It was all the boys could do to keep from busting a gut laughing.

Sherry walked out into the yard. "Hi." She smiled.

The man jumped back. "Who are you?"

"I live here," Sherry smiled.

"What's making that terrible noise?" the woman asked.

"Oh," Sherry paused, tryin' to come up with a scary monster name, "that was just the land shark fightin' with the man-eatees."

"A what?" exclaimed the man.

"Pull it," whispered Larry, and the screamer roared again.

The man lost his balance when his wife and kids grabbed him at the same time. With children hanging on both legs, his pants had slipped down to his knees. Sherry politely turned away so as not to see his undies.

"Them land sharks are very dangerous," Sherry nodded. "They ate the people who used to live here before."

"Ate them!" the woman said, putting her hand over her heart.

"That's right," Sherry said, kicking her toe in the dust. "And the man-eatees ate the last man who came lookin' at our house."

"Let's leave now," the woman said, taking her children by the hand.

"Let's pull it just one more time," Terry said, giving it a tug.

The mountain screamer roared. The man was halfway into his automobile when his children jumped up and pulled his pants down again. He managed to get everyone into the car and gunned the engine, driving away with his pants still down.

When they were out of sight, Larry and Terry came out, leaving the mountain screamer behind the barn. "You were great!" Terry said, slapping Sherry on the back.

"Tellin' 'em it was land sharks. I thought I'd wet my pants," Larry laughed. The mountain screamer roared again and Larry turned to Terry. "Quit pullin' it."

"I ain't pullin' it. We left it behind the barn," said Terry.

Six Youngun eyebrows raised in the air as the screamer roared again. "Let's get outta here!" Terry shouted, running down the road.

Maurice came out laughing from behind the barn, but his laughter. turned to tears. *I sure will miss playin' tricks on them. I need to talk to someone,* he thought. *I need to talk to Blindman.*

CHAPTER 36

THE GIFT

$\mathbb{M}$aurice was so depressed that he felt he was going crazy. That little practical joke on the Younguns had set it all off again.

The thought of their moving away had gotten out of hand. Maurice had lost all perspective about it and now was at the point where he couldn't handle it.

"Where you goin'?" Eulla Mae called after him as he stepped out the front door.

"Goin' for a walk. Got some thinkin' to do," Maurice said sullenly.

Eulla Mae watched him. *If I'd have been able to have children, he wouldn't be feelin' like this. He'd have his own children to love, instead of them three.* She closed the door and leaned against it with tears in her eyes. Tears for what her husband was going through and tears for the family they would never have.

Ain't fair! A man with as much love to give as Maurice not havin' children to give it to. He needs his own kids, not someone else's. Then Eulla Mae shook her head.

When he got to Blindman's, Maurice just took the latchkey off the nail and started to open the door.

"Who's that?" Blindman called out.

"It's Maurice, a hungry neighbor comin' to visit."

"You don't need the key," Blindman laughed. "I never lock the door."

"Thought you told me to use the latchkey," Maurice said, hanging it back on the nail.

"Too hard for me to get the key in the hole. Anyway, if a robber come in here, I couldn't see him anyway, so he'd have a fine ol' time walkin' off with everythin' but Gertie here."

"Gertie?" Maurice said, looking around.

"My harmonica," Blindman laughed, playing a quick riff of blues. "Now, what's on your mind?"

"Said I'm a hungry neighbor. Ain't this what you wanted?"

"You mean you comin' round to eat me out of house and home?" Blindman laughed.

"No sir! You said that I should learn to take time to make time. That's what I'm doin'."

Blindman shook his head. "You ain't doin' no such thing. You still got a worried mind."

"If you don't want me 'round, just say so," Maurice said with false indignation.

"Sit down, ya old fool. You come to talk, so talk."

Maurice paused, then started talking about what wasn't on his mind. "I just wanted to understand why I'm poor and feelin' poorly."

Blindman chuckled. "Poor? You think I'm rich or something'? I'm rich up here," he said, tapping his forehead. "But poor, why you can put that at the bottom of life's list, just ahead of sick and dead." He shook his head. "For a man with good health, workin' arms, and legs and eyes that can see ol' Blindman, you sure are a sorry cuss."

"These are bad times for me, Blindman," Maurice whispered.

"Son, you listen to this old man. The times past that you thinkin' of, and the times to come that you thinkin' you lost, are no better than the times you got now. You understand? What's gonna happen good is what good you make happen."

Maurice put his hands to his face. "Eulla Mae, she couldn't have no children, so these Youngun kids have sort of become my kids and—"

"You on the edge," Blindman said quietly.

Maurice nodded. "I feel like I'm a-goin' crazy. I'm losin' my mind over them three kids leavin'."

Blindman moved his chair closer to Maurice and took his hand. "Look into my eyes," he commanded. Maurice gulped and looked away. "I said, look into my eyes."

Maurice looked into the cloudy, sightless eyes. "I am," he whispered.

"Good. Now you listen up and listen good. 'Cause you, you're standin' knee-deep in the river of life and dyin' of thirst." His cloudy, vacant eyes looked around. "Are you listenin'?"

"Yes . . . yes sir," Maurice answered, mesmerized by the eyes.

"Sometimes you got to go a little crazy to keep from goin' all-the-way crazy, to keep from goin' over the edge. You understand?"

"I'm tryin' to," Maurice whispered.

"Ain't nothin' wrong with a man cryin'. Heck, we all got fears and tears hid up inside us, 'cept that we've been told that cryin's for babies and women. But that's wrong. That's why men go crazy and do crazy things."

Blindman could sense the tears building up and then the flow. "That's good. Let 'em come," he whispered to Maurice. He squeezed Maurice's hands, then let go and picked up his harmonica. "Gertie wants to talk to you," he said, then began softly blowing a tune.

Maurice closed his eyes, humming to the sweet gospel music that seemed to climb up the stairs of his mind, smoothing out the rough edges. From the other room, Maurice heard Reever's voice sing the chorus.

> That's the way God planned our lives.
> He knows who'll live and he knows who'll die.
> But the plans God made tore my life apart.
> Taking you away just broke my heart and,
> That's the way God planned our lives to be.

Maurice kept the tune going for a while. Blindman spoke in soft sentences. "Yes sir, Maurice, you're gonna get through this. I know you will. Good Lord knows what you're feelin' . . . knows the love in your heart. And that's why you should give those kids a special gift when they leave."

Maurice kept humming, but had questions in his eyes. Blindman smiled. "I can feel the questions."

"What special gift can I give them?" Maurice whispered.

Blindman squeezed his hands again. "You got to give them somethin' from your heart."

"But what?"

"You'll know," Blindman said softly. "You'll know what to give from your heart when the time comes."

Blindman put his harmonica to his lips and began playing. Maurice closed his eyes and hummed along, searching his heart for the gift he could leave the Younguns with.

CHAPTER 37

TELEGRAM

The next day, at a special Thanksgiving service, the town had a lot to be thankful for. A sense of calm had come over the town. Reason and goodwill prevailed.

With Rev. Youngun set to get married the next day and then leave for Florida, it was a packed, farewell service for him and his family. He looked out over his congregation, nodded to Carla and his children and just talked from his heart.

"One of the things I've tried to do at this church is to help create an atmosphere where it's everybody's church. I wanted a church that belonged to anyone and everyone."

He paused and smiled. "I know many of you are sad that we're leaving. And believe me, my children and I are going to shed a lot of tears when we say good-bye. But God has given me a mission and there is no way I can avoid it. I have to plunge ahead with my life and do whatever he has planned for me."

Rev. Youngun smiled, holding back a tear. "You see, the good Lord is always leading us on a trail from where we are to the place God wants us to be. Sometimes the road seems to go in circles and sometimes it doesn't seem to make a whole lot of sense. My trail leads to Florida now, to take on another challenge and build another church.

"If there is anything, I can leave you with, it's this," he said, looking at Chan and the other two Chinese families sitting in the front row. "The real spirit of America and good fellowship is in this room. It is the spirit of people just like ourselves and people who are different. But we or our relatives all came to America for the same reason, and thus have become one people with a lot of different faces. And that is what makes us great."

He held his hands up in the air and said, "If we can broaden our vision to see the world as a whole, we will know that this is what makes people into good friends and neighbors. If we truly open our hearts, we will realize that never again can we be strangers."

After a moment of silence, he bowed his head and said, "I'd like everyone here to say a prayer for Laura Ingalls Wilder, who is struggling not to lose the baby inside her."

The entire congregation bowed their heads in prayer, and after the service, Manly came up and shook his hand. "Rev. Youngun, that was mighty nice of you."

"How is she?" Rev. Youngun asked.

Manly shook his head. "She's over at the hotel, where the Doc put her when they brought her in. Doc says it's touch and go. She took a bad fall on her stomach and seemed to mess a few things up."

"We're all praying for them both," Rev. Youngun said, squeezing Manly's hand.

"I best be gettin' back to the hotel now," Manly said and turned to go.

Carla came up from behind and took Rev. Youngun's hand. "I think it's wonderful that the whole town is pitching in to have a big Thanksgiving for the Chinese at the hotel."

"It's the least we can do after what they've been through."

"And it saves us from having to cook a big meal at the house. We've got enough to do with all the packing."

"Where are the kids?" he asked.

"Maurice wanted to take them for a ride. He said he had something he wanted to give them as a going away present."

Rev. Youngun shook his head. "That man's hurtin' in his heart. It hasn't hit the kids how much they're gonna miss him."

Stephen Scales, the telegraph operator, came up with a glum face. "Got a message for you," he said to Carla.

"For me?" she smiled. "I wonder who's sending congratulations now?"

"This is the day before my wedding. Couldn't it have waited until tomorrow after the wedding?" Rev. Youngun asked.

Scales shrugged. "This one's kind of important," he said, looking down. Then he turned to leave.

"You must have already gotten twenty weddin' cards." Rev. Youngun smiled, shaking his head at the beauty of his wife-to-be.

ASIAN-PACIFIC TRADING COMPANY

To: Carla Pobst

Your husband, John Pobst, has been picked up by one of our ships in the Pacific. He is in good health, considering the small island he has survived on for the past two years. He sends you his love and asks that you meet him in San Francisco when he docks there around December 15 at our wharf.

Manager
APTC

Carla read it again and grabbed her heart. "Oh no!" she moaned, feeling faint.

"What's wrong?" Rev. Youngun asked, putting his arm around her. "Did someone die?"

The tears streamed down her face. She looked at Rev. Youngun, then back at the telegraph message. "Someone's come back from the dead," she said, handing it to him to read.

While Rev. Youngun read it, Carla slipped off the engagement ring that he'd given her, placed it in his hand, and walked from the church. Lost in a sea of tears, conflicting emotions, she didn't know how she should react to the message that the husband she had buried in her mind had come back.

But she knew that the wedding would have to be canceled and she had to get away from Mansfield. Rev. Youngun put down the telegram. He felt as if a knife was ripping out his heart.

"Carla? Where's Carla?" he asked frantically.

He saw her running toward town and the hotel and took off after her. "Carla, wait!" he shouted, stumbling several times in the blindness of his tears.

Grabbing her arm, he spun her around. "We've got to talk. You can get a divorce."

Carla shook her head. "I don't believe in it, and neither do you. But I love you." She looked into his eyes, neither one able to hold back the tears. "I wanted to marry you, Thomas. I wanted to spend my life with you. Have your babies and—"

"And you still can," he said, smoothing her hair. "You still can. I don't want to ever let you go."

Carla shook her head. "I've got to go back to Cape. I've got to get away to think."

"But what about Florida?"

"We've each got to go where God leads us," she said, half-heartedly.

"But I'll go to San Francisco with you. Explain things to him and—"

"Explain what? That I thought he was dead, fell in love with someone else and planned to remarry and have children by another man?"

Rev. Youngun dropped her hands, seeing the craziness of the situation.

"I've got to go, Thomas. I've got to go," she said, walking away.

Rev. Youngun was wracked by sobs, unable to stop the flood of emotions. He had signed over his house for William Bentley to sell. He had accepted the church assignment in Florida. And he was moving in two days.

My life is ruined, he thought. *I have nothing without Carla.*

CHAPTER 38

GOOD-BYE, KIDS

Maurice and the three Younguns rode with breaking hearts in his wagon on the road home. All the children could do was cling to his arms, crying.

"Please come with us," Sherry begged.

"We love you," Larry cried.

"You're my best friend," Terry said, feeling that his whole world was coming apart.

"Kids . . . kids, there's nothin' I can do. Your daddy's got to go where God's callin' him and—"

Terry interrupted. "I wish God would call someone else."

"I know," Maurice said, smoothing Terry's auburn hair, "but you kids are goin' to be movin', and I got somethin' for you."

"What is it?" Terry asked, looking around the wagon. "Ain't nothin' in here."

Maurice chuckled. "Terry, you'll never change, you know it?"

"What'd you get us?" Sherry asked.

"I just wanted to tell you a few things to remember as you grow up," he said. He stopped the wagon and looked into their eyes. "First of all, I don't want any of you hangin' round with bad people. You remember what Maurice tells you. You're known by the people you hang around. Promise me you'll remember that," he commanded.

"I promise," they chorused back through their tears.

"And always remember that you have to stand for somethin' good in your life or you'll just fall for anythin' that comes along. Don't be a follower. I think each of you kids has the makins of a leader . . . and don't you forget it. Promise me."

"Promise," sniffed Sherry, hugging onto his arm.

"We promise," Terry and Larry said.

"And another thing, you kids have a streak of mischief in you, but I also know that you got kind hearts. I want you to remember that you should never lose the magic of bein' a child. Don't let anyone wash it out of you. That way you'll never really grow old in your mind. Hold onto bein' a child and keep it a secret from the rest of the world."

The Younguns nodded. "And don't be braggarts. You don't need to tell people good things you done. 'Cause if you do them from your heart, that's all the praise and thanks you need."

He paused, wiping back a tear. "True greatness, which is the measure of a person, comes in the little things we do that no one sees. You understand me, children?"

The Younguns nodded together, each one rubbing the tears from their eyes. Maurice hugged them for a moment, then took a deep breath.

"And now I want to give you somethin'." Six Youngun eyes followed his hands. "I got it in my pockets . . . just special for you all," he said, sticking his right hand deep in.

"Ah, here it is," he said, cupping his hands together so they couldn't see inside.

"This is somethin' that I'm goin' to give each of you. It's better than gold or diamonds, 'cause this is somethin' that can't be bought," he said, lifting up his cupped hands.

"What is it?" Terry asked.

"Terry, what I got inside here will help you when you feel the world is against you. It'll smooth out some of the problems you might encounter just because you're redheaded and smaller than the rest. What you got inside this head of yours are brains. You got brains, and nothin' can stop a man who can think for himself."

"And Sherry," he smiled, kissing her cheek. "What I got inside here will help you become someone special. By the time you grow up, it's gonna be a whole new world out there. Ain't nobody gonna hold you back 'cause you're a girl."

He paused and smiled. "And Larry, what I got in here will give you the strength to be the man you are. To not be scared of no one, but at the same time, not ever feelin' you need to use your physical strength against someone for no good reason."

He paused, then said, "Hold out your hands."

The Younguns held out their hands, hanging on his every word. They watched in awed silence as Maurice opened his hands. There was nothing there except ten, old, black, knarled fingers hooked together.

"What I got for each of you is invisible love," he said, pouring a little of it into each of their outstretched hands. "Now drink it," he commanded. "Now put some of your love

into my hands," he whispered as he began to cry unstoppable tears.

The Younguns did as he commanded. He put his lips to his hands and pretended to drink it down.

"Now you remember, all you have to do is believe. I'll always be there with you when you need me. That's the power of invisible love. When you close your eyes and think that life's problems got you down, just think about ol' Maurice, and I'll be there smilin' in front of you to help you make it through."

To any passersby, it would have seemed strange to see the big black man and the three little white children hugging and crying together. But that's because they couldn't see the invisible love that they'd shared together.

CHAPTER 39

THANKSGIVING

Manly sat beside Laura's bed in the hotel. "Wish you could come down to see the Thanksgivin' spread. It looks like a feast for a king."

"I wish I could," Laura whispered, "but I keep having pains." She fingered the locket that Chan had given her. "Grandmother Chan told me that this symbol means good luck in Chinese," she said, showing him the locket.

Dr. George sat on the other side. "That fall pushed the baby down. Thought she was gonna deliver earlier there for a while."

"Want me to bring you up a plate of food?" Manly asked. Laura shook her head no. "How 'bout some peaches?" He smiled.

"I'm just not hungry," she said, closing her eyes. "I'm kind of tired."

"She needs some rest," Dr. George said. "Come on, let's you and I go on down and eat." He turned to the housemaid who was to watch Laura. "You keep an eye on her and come get me if anythin' at all happens, you hear?"

"Yes, doctor," the maid said.

* * *

The dining room of the hotel was crowded with the people of Mansfield. Blindman sat with Grandmother Chan in the corner as they played their harps.

Harmonica Preston came up to them. "I still want to find who's better on the harp. You ready now?"

Blindman laughed. "We don't need no contest."

"We don't? Why not?" Harmonica asked suspiciously.

"'Cause you're better than I am, and that's that."

Harmonica was dumbfounded. "Why didn't you tell me that before?"

Blindman chuckled. "Just a fact of life that youth can do better things than the old folks. But that's somethin' you'll understand when you get older."

"But why didn't you tell me? It would have saved a lot of arguing."

"I would have told you before, but I was waitin' for the common sense in your head to catch up with your playin' mouth."

Maurice brought the Younguns into the room. "Where's Pa?" Larry asked.

Stephen Scales took Maurice aside and told him about the telegraph message. "Anybody know where he is?" Maurice asked.

"Lafayette said he saw him walkin' up toward the Willow Creek Bridge. Said Rev. Youngun didn't even recognize him. Said he looked in a daze."

Maurice walked over to his wife. "Eulla Mae, you watch out for these kids. I gotta hurry."

* * *

At the Willow Creek Bridge, Rev. Youngun looked down into the deep, black water. *I love Carla. Why'd her husband have to come back? Why'd he have to ruin my life? Why couldn't he have stayed where he was?*

He felt guilty at what he was feeling, and looked again at the note that Carla had left for him at the hotel.

Dearest Thomas,

I thought I knew the worst of pain, when I first heard that John had supposedly died. I thought I'd reached the bottom of my heart. But I didn't know how much farther I had to fall until I fell in love with you and now have to say good-bye.

You'll always be with me in my heart and soul. No matter what happens in my life, no one can take the special place in my heart that you occupy. I want you to know that each night, when I say my prayers, I'll be with you again. Each knock I hear at my door, I'll be wishing, hoping that it's you, but I know that it will never be.

Though we'll never be married, never share a new home together, or have the children we planned, I want you to know something. You will always be on my mind—forever.

I love you.
Carla

Rev. Youngun looked down in the water, feeling it calling out to him. *What do I have to live for?* he thought, over and over.

"A wise old man told me that sometime you got to go a little bit crazy to keep from goin' all the way crazy," Maurice said quietly to his friend.

Rev. Youngun was startled. "What are you doin' here?" he asked defensively.

"I been lookin' for you. Heard you got yourself a bad, bad message."

Rev. Youngun nodded and handed it to Maurice.

Maurice read it and whistled. "You got yourself into one heck of a fix."

Rev. Youngun turned around, his eyes red and swollen from crying. "I loved her. I've got a right to happiness. I've got a right to a life besides raising children."

Maurice put his arm around his friend, sensing the pain in his heart. "I know that sometimes it probably seems that you're raisin' Cain instead of raisin' children, but that's 'cause they're special." He paused, nodding to his friend. "Ah-huh, that's right. Them special kids need you. They ain't got a momma, and what would they do without a daddy? Go to the orphanage?"

Rev. Youngun looked down into the water and saw his reflection. *You'll survive,* it seemed to say to him. *You'll get through this because you have to. You have no other choice.*

Maurice pulled him along. "I think we need to go eat that Thanksgivin' dinner. What do you say?"

Rev. Youngun nodded, and walked along. He knew he had taken the longest step of his life and landed on safe ground.

"You still don't have to move away," Maurice said quietly.

"Where would we live?" Rev. Youngun asked.

"Why, at your home."

"I shook hands with a man at the service today who came from Springfield to buy the house. Said he just wants to see it one more time this afternoon."

"Then you'll stay if he doesn't buy it?"

Rev. Youngun nodded. "I don't want to leave my friends and my town. It's all I got . . . besides my kids." Then he shook his head. "But I don't think there's a chance in the world that he won't buy it."

"I'll talk to the kids about it," Maurice mumbled.

"What?" Rev. Youngun asked.

"Oh, nothin'," Maurice smiled.

They entered the hotel quietly. Dr. George nodded as he walked past them to check on Laura.

Taking their seats, Rev. Youngun looked into the faces of his children and hugged them. "I love you," he said to them all.

Manly stood in the front of the room and spoke to the crowd. He thanked the women of the town for all their efforts and acknowledged the Chinese guests, who sat by his side. Tong squeezed Yu-Lan's hand, excited over all the people in the room.

Manly spoke. "America is not a single color or religion. That's somethin' they ought to put on the Statue of Liberty. America is a state of mind. I want you to know that it's that feelin', that yearnin' in your mind that brings the best people in the world to America. And though we got more colors than a rainbow, we are truly one people, united by the land we've all come to.

"Now, I'd like Rev. Youngun to say grace," he said, nodding to Rev. Youngun.

"Would you mind if I say it?" Chan asked.

"No. Would you mind, Thomas?" Manly asked. Rev. Youngun shook his head.

Chan stood and bowed his head. He said a prayer in Chinese, then repeated it in English. Then he asked everyone to join hands and sing "Amazing Grace." "I want everyone in the land of promise to sing as they feel."

It was a moving experience for everyone in the room, with the song sung in English, Chinese, and the accents of the immigrants from around the world, putting their own conviction in the hymn.

"Mr. Wilder, come quick!" shouted the maid who'd been assisting Dr. George.

"What's wrong?" Manly asked, walking to the door.

"Dr. George says you better get upstairs."

"Did somethin' happen to Laura?"

"She had herself a baby. A baby girl," the maid smiled.

CHAPTER 40

YOUNGUNS IN ACTION!

Larry looked at his brother and sister. They were wearing their Sunday best and the stiff collars hurt their necks. "Maurice said it wouldn't be right to trick the man."

"Why can't we just tell him to go home?" Sherry asked.

"'Cause Pa said that he shook on the deal," Larry said.

"Well, the deal's shakin' me up," Terry frowned.

"Can't we just start cryin' and kickin' the walls?" Sherry asked.

"We promised Pa we'd be little angels," Terry said and made a face. "This bein' an angel business has made me hungry," he said, opening up the ice box.

"Make yourself a sandwich," Sherry said.

"Why don't you make me somethin' to eat?"

"Quit bein' lazy," Larry said.

"Can't help it if I'm hungry," Terry said.

"You want some popcorn?" Sherry asked.

"Do we got any popcorn, Sherry?" Larry asked, rummaging in the pantry.

"Yeah," Sherry said, "but Pa don't know how to make it."

"Show me where it is," Larry said. Sherry showed him the

five-pound paper sack marked "Popping Corn." "How do you make popcorn?" Larry asked his brother.

"I don't know." Terry shrugged.

"I know, I know!" Sherry exclaimed.

"You do? Who taught you?" Larry asked, suspiciously.

Sherry did a strutted in a small circle. "Learned it watchin' the man make popcorn at the carnival."

"What time's the man supposed to come look at the house again?" Terry asked.

"I think in 'bout half an hour," Terry said.

"Is that enough time to make popcorn?" Larry asked Sherry.

"Sure! I can make a bunch up and have the kitchen cleaned up before that mean old man gets here."

Terry liked the idea. "I want my popcorn with butter and salt. You know how to make it with butter and salt?"

"Sure, sure. Let me make it and surprise you, okay?"

Larry said, "It's okay with me. Just don't make a mess, okay? Pa will get steamin' mad if we mess up his handshake."

"I never make messes. Only Terry does." She smirked and stuck out her tongue at Terry.

Terry jumped toward her and Larry grabbed his arm. "We'll be out messin' around in the barn. You bring out the bowl of popcorn when you're ready. You know how to light the stove?"

"Would you do it?"

"Sure," Larry said, getting out a long, wooden kitchen match. He struck it against the bottom of his shoe and lit the stove. "Be careful and don't burn yourself."

"Okay." Sherry smiled. "It'll only take a minute."

"Remember, lots of butter," Terry said, walking out the door.

Sherry slapped her hands together, then began making popcorn. Dragging a chair over to the stove, she held her hand over the burner to make sure it was nice and hot.

From the pantry, she got out the turkey roaster and put it on the stove. Then she took out a two pound block of butter from the ice box and dropped it into the roaster and watched it melt.

When it was crackling, she took a coffee cup and began putting in the popping corn . . . all five pounds of it. Then she added a bag of salt and put the lid tightly on the turkey roaster.

Sitting down on the chair to wait for the corn to pop, she slapped her hands. "Nothin' to it."

Pulling into the driveway, the man said to his wife and children, "Now, keep away from these kids here. They tricked us before."

"They frightened the children," his wife said.

"Can I hit 'em if they get near me?" his son asked.

"No, their father promised me that they'd be little angels. Those were his exact words. Little angels." He gunned the car forward. "Now, let's go see if we want to buy this house. This is our last look."

In the barn, Larry tried to get Dangit to sit up, which was useless. "He's a dumb smart dog," Larry said, shaking his head.

"I agree," Terry said. Crab Apple the mule hee-hawed. Lightning the horse whinnied. Little Bessie the pig grunted, and Teddy Roosevelt the turkey was gobbled around in circles.

"I think they agree it's hopeless," Larry said. he sat down by the horse trough. "Can you think of a way to get him to sit up?"

Beezer the parrot came walking into the barn. "Furget it! Say your prayers!"

"That's all we need," Terry said, "a talking green bird tellin' us what to do!"

"You're pathetic!" Beezer squawked.

Larry glanced toward the house. "I wonder how Sherry's comin' with the popcorn?"

Terry laughed. "I'll be surprised if she even gets one to pop."

"Hope she makes a lot of it," Larry said. "Cause I'm gettin' hungry."

The man and his family stopped in front of the Younguns' house. "This is a wonderful place. So quiet," he said to his family.

"I bet if we closed our eyes we could hear a pin drop," his wife said, squeezing his hand.

In the kitchen, Sherry was sitting on the chair, swinging her legs. Suddenly she heard the first popping sounds and smiled.

"Almost ready. Hope there'll be enough for all of us."

Pop . . . pop pop . . . pop pop pop pop pop pop pop . . . pop pop popopopopopopopopopopop! It sounded like a hail storm on a tin roof!

Sherry was really happy now and wanted to sneak a peek and stood up on the chair. With a thick pot holder she lifted the lid just a bit and was knocked from the chair by a barrage of flying popcorn! The lid fell off and popped popcorn flew everywhere.

"Help!" she screamed. "Larry, help me! Stop the corn!"

"What was that?" the man asked from the front of the house.

"Sounded like a little girl screaming. You better check," she told her husband.

Larry cocked his head to the sound in the barn. "What was that?"

Terry shrugged. "Just Sherry screaming some nonsense 'bout stoppin' corn."

"Help!" she screamed again from the kitchen.

"Come on," Larry said, taking off on a run, "maybe she hurt herself on the stove!"

The two brothers ran up the back stairs and into a blizzard of hot, popping popcorn flying through the air! Sherry hid under the kitchen table with a pot over her head.

"Looks like a war!" Larry shouted. He ducked as a hundred pieces came toward his face.

Terry opened his mouth and caught one and chewed it. "Not enough butter," he said.

Larry tossed him a pot lid. "Put it on and get down."

They crawled to where Sherry lay under the table. An inch of popcorn covered the kitchen and more fell around them every second.

The man who wanted to buy the house rushed into the kitchen and slid on the stick of butter that had melted on the floor. "What in tarnation?" he said, trying to pick the buttery popcorn off his clothes.

"You hungry?" Terry asked.

"Am I . . ." the man couldn't finish his sentence. His mouth had filled up with popcorn.

Then his wife and children came running in and slipped on the buttery floor. In their efforts to stand up amid the blizzard of popcorn, they managed to knock the honey jar off the shelf and ended up looking like snowmen.

"You can tell your father that we will *not* buy his house!" the man shouted, then stormed off with his family in tow. The Younguns broke into cheers.

"Looks like we ain't movin!" Terry shouted. The kids hugged each other, then tossed popcorn around the room.

Sherry squealed for joy, then looked at the mess in the kitchen. "Looks like we're in trouble . . . big trouble."

Dangit scratched open the back door. Larry shouted, "Dangit, stop there, sit!" Dangit sat down and opened his mouth, catching a dozen pieces of popcorn. He chewed them greedily and caught some more.

"We got to get rid of this 'fore Pa gets home," said Sherry.

"Pa's gonna whup us for sure," Terry moaned as the popping corn began to die down. Terry looked around. "The only thing we can do is . . . start eatin'!" He stuffed his mouth and began chewing as fast as he could.

Sherry began crying. "We can't eat all this popcorn!"

Terry thought the problem was with the cook. "There'stoomuchpopcorn . . . andnotenoughbutter!"

Larry was disgusted. "Don't talk with your mouth full."

Terry gulped down a mouthful. "Sorry . . . but we can't eat all this stuff." He looked around the room. "It looks like it snowed in here."

Dangit ate popcorn as fast as he could. Sherry laughed. "Maybe Dangit can eat it all!"

Larry got an idea. "Terry, go get Little Bessie, T.R., and Bashful. They can eat up this stuff."

Sherry ran along with Terry to the barn. She picked up the piglet and Terry shooed the turkey along. "Where's Bashful?" he screamed, looking for the goat who had fainted behind him. "You're worthless," he said to the goat. "Come on T.R. We got somethin' good for you to eat!"

Crab Apple switched his tail and backed out of his stall. They'd left the barn door open, so he slowly wandered out in the sunlight, sniffing the air.

Little Bessie began eating as fast as she could, and Teddy Roosevelt gobbled and pecked the ones on top of the chairs. The Younguns filled pots and pans with popcorn and dumped it on a blanket by the door.

Hee-haw . . . hee-haw.

The Younguns stopped. Crab Apple stuck his head through the kitchen doorway. He opened his mouth and it was stuffed with popcorn!

Larry laughed. "Crab Apple's eaten every piece on the blanket. Keep fillin' it up!"

It was a noisy eat-and-clean team, but after ten minutes, Little Bessie and Dangit rolled over on their sides, stuffed with popcorn. "They're full as ticks," Terry said in amazement.

Bessie walked sideways. Larry laughed. "She's a real stuffed pig!"

Dangit was full that he didn't put up any resistance when Larry dumped him in the sink. Teddy Roosevelt let out a loud turkey burp, and Crab Apple looked as if he might not keep his snack down.

Larry's mouth hung open. The image of Crab Apple getting sick on the floor was too much. "Come on, Crabbie!" he yelled, pulling him back to the barn. He came back to the kitchen, out of breath. "Terry, you carry Little Bessie, and I'll drag Dangit out. Pa will know fursure that we done somethin' if he sees them passed out from eatin'."

When they got back to the kitchen, Sherry was sitting in the middle of a popcorn pile, crying her eyes out. The animals had eaten a lot, but not nearly enough. She looked at the popcorn-covered room. "Where are we gonna hide this stuff? Can't throw it in the yard."

Larry put some popcorn in his mouth and chewed while he thought. "Let me think about it."

Terry arched his eyes. "We can't eat all the evidence. We'll bust a gut."

"No, can't do that," Larry said with a mouthful of popcorn.

Terry shook his head. "Can't just drop it in the yard. It'll look like it snowed."

Larry agreed. "But we have to hide it someplace. Someplace where it'll never be seen."

"Where?" Terry asked.

"Give it to Faithful," Sherry grinned. "He'll eat anythin'."

"What?" Terry asked. "Give it to who?"

"Drop it in Old Faithful," she smiled, taking the pot off her head.

"That's a great idea!" Larry exclaimed, thinking about dropping the popcorn into the outhouse. "Come on, let's clean this mess up," Larry said.

It took four blanket loads to get it all to the outhouse and another ten minutes for the flock of blackbirds to eat all the popcorn they'd dropped along the way.

At the outhouse Larry had written "No Girls in Here" on his half-door. Terry had written "Do Not Enner," and Sherry had painted a flower on hers. They'd named it "Old Faithful" and scrawled on the side, "Come and drop in." They used it for hide-and-seek, lookout posts and a convenient place to drop the vegetables that they cupped in napkins when they asked to be excused from the dinner table.

By the time Rev. Youngun got home, the kitchen was cleaned and the three Younguns were sittin' in their three-hole privy as if nothing had happened.

As their father walked up Terry looked down the hole and whispered to Larry, "I just hope none of that popcorn pops back up now."

Rev. Youngun grinned when he saw his three children sittin' there, lined up behind their swinging half-doors. "Did you hear the good news? The man's not goin' to buy the house!" He shook his head. "But I can't for the life of me figure out what he meant by a snowstorm in the kitchen."

"Maybe he was crazy," Terry said.

"Does that mean we can stay?" Larry asked.

"It sure does," Rev. Youngun smiled.

"But I wanted to see the ocean," Sherry said, her lips puckering up.

"Hush up!" Larry whispered.

"We'll, you're in luck," Rev. Youngun smiled, walking away. "Because we're goin' down to Jacksonville to visit. They invited me to come down and preach for a few weeks. I think the vacation will do us all good."

"I thought we were movin' fursure," Larry said to his brother and sister.

"I never worried 'bout it for a moment," Terry said. "I knew we'd think of somethin'."

"Why didn't you worry?" Sherry asked.

"'Cause we're the Younguns," Terry smiled. "Come on, let's go on inside. I got some candy I want to celebrate with."

CHAPTER 41

LAND OF PROMISE

Dr. George said he'd never seen a quicker delivery in his life. As he sat in the parlor of Apple Hill Farm a week later, he smiled at Laura and her new baby girl.

"I mean to tell you, one minute you were complainin' that your stomach hurt, and the next minute you were deliverin'."

Laura kissed the baby's cheeks and smiled. "And you didn't get to eat your Thanksgiving dinner."

"This will be a Thanksgiving I'll never forget," he laughed.

Manly smiled. "You knew it was a girl, didn't you?"

Laura nodded. "I just had this feeling," she said, nuzzling the baby. "I just had this feeling that Little Laurie was inside there."

"New life's a wonderful thing," Dr. George smiled.

"All life is wonderful," Laura whispered.

"Amen," said Manly.

"And Little Laurie's going to have a wonderful life," Laura whispered, kissing the baby's cheek again. "She's going to make a name for herself. I can just feel it."

"Maybe she'll be a writer, just like you," Manly smiled.

"You never know," Laura said.

On the other side of the country, the cab stopped at the edge of the Jacksonville, Florida, beach. The three Younguns got out and stared.

"What's that?" Sherry asked.

"That's the ocean," Rev. Youngun smiled. The three children backed up. "What's wrong? Don't you want to touch the water."

Sherry whimpered as she looked around. "Don't let the land sharks get me."

"Watch out for sea-needles," Terry said, raising his feet.

"You kids have wild imaginations," Rev. Youngun said. "Take your shoes off and follow me. You've got nothing to worry about."

At the water's edge, the Younguns thought they'd never seen anything more amazing in their lives. "It's bigger than Mansfield," Terry whispered.

"It's bigger than all the land in the world," Rev. Youngun said. "You kids stay right here. I've got somethin' I need to do."

He walked down the beach, looking for a bottle. Finding the right one, he took Carla's letter and stuffed it inside, sealed it with the lump of wax he'd brought along, and heaved the bottle out to sea.

As it bobbed away, he closed his eyes. *He was lost and found at sea. That is the story of my love for you, Carla. You will always be on my mind.*

Sherry began crying. "What's wrong?" Larry asked.

"I miss Maurice."

"So do I," Terry whimpered.

"Take some of this," Larry said, cupping his hands. They all reached in for a bit of Maurice's invisible love. "All you have to do is believe," Larry whispered. And for a moment, it seemed Maurice was right there, smiling in front of them.

Invisible love. Giving from your heart. Accepting others for what they are. That's all part of the land of promise.

What happened in Mansfield, Missouri was part of the spirit of America. People coming together, overcoming difficulties, forging one nation. New life being welcomed into the family, the family of all the people of the world.

And somewhere in the Ozarks, perhaps the music made by an old black man and a Chinese woman is still floating through the hills, calling us together. And in the clouds you might see a multicolored kite or hear the Pledge of Allegiance spoken by the children of the Ozarks.

It's all a part of The Days of Laura Ingalls Wilder.

ABOUT THE AUTHOR

T.L. Tedrow is a bestselling author, screenwriter, and film producer. His books include the eight-book "Days of Laura Ingalls Wilder Series": *Missouri Homestead, Children of Promise, Good Neighbors, Home to the Prairie, The World's Fair, Mountain Miracle, The Great Debate,* and *Land of Promise,* which are the basis of a new television series. His eight-book series on "The Younguns," to be released in 1993, has also been sold as a television series. He lives with his wife, Carla, and their four children in Winter Park, Florida.